BRITISH

VAMPIRE ASSASSIN
LEAGUE

INCLUDES:
ANYONE HERE
THIS VAMPIRE AS

Jackie Ivie

A Vampire Assassin League
Novella

THIS VAMPIRE
AS

JACKIE IVIE

CHAPTER ONE

They just did not make warriors like they used to. Or whatever they called fighting men in these modern licentious times. Bad guys. Opposing forces. Hordes. Troops. Adversaries. Foes. Enemies.

No. Wait.

That was too harsh. One had to have been in contact with someone in order to call them an enemy. That should be listed in his chivalric code. If not, he'd ponder with adding it…when he returned to his crypt and had nothing better to do. In the meantime, whatever he deemed these combatants, they made lousy warriors and worse knights. They'd probably never even heard of chivalry.

Too bad. Chivalrous behavior was Wystan's creed. His motto. His reason for living. His—

Wystan shook his head. Why was he wasting time on such thoughts? So what if chivalry was dead? So was he.

He pulled his sword from Body Number Six.

Oh. Damn. Look there.

He'd nicked a large vein. That was messy. Wystan sidestepped the gush of fluid, coming in spurts that matched tempo with a dying heart. This particular man had barely lasted ten seconds. That's what came of answering Wystan's appearance and hissed challenge with an exclamation, followed by a taser hit, and when that didn't work, bringing out a gun equipped with a silencer. Not one of these men carried a sword. Wasn't a sword a requirement anymore? When had that changed? And was he really that far behind the times?

Hmm. They really should be carrying swords.

The ring of steel on steel was bound to bring some notice, and maybe some back-up, and maybe they'd last a bit longer and give a little better fight. Then again, maybe no one thought it necessary. That showed one of two things – either they hadn't done their research or they were extremely arrogant and self-assured. No back-up in place. No warning system. Nothing but a few armed men spaced a hundred feet or so apart, and each one equipped with silent weaponry. That made it an easy matter to infiltrate deeper and deeper into the abandoned ruin that was called Rockcliffe Castle. Kidnappers should know better than to hold a scared, little, six-year-old girl in a big old gloomy castle and not have some sort of alarm system in place.

Maybe they actually thought the Carlotti patriarch would pay.

Wystan shook his head again. Forget the arrogance. They were apparently very short-sighted. And ill-informed. If you took a Carlotti grandchild from the back of a staged play in what was supposed to be an exclusive, *guarded* school, and then managed to spirit her out of the country in order to hold her for ransom, you should probably have done some homework on contacts and recent history.

The Carlotti family wasn't paying three-point-six million in ransom money. They preferred to spend that exact amount in the hit. And they knew exactly who to call. All of which should have clued Wystan in on the lack of chivalry attached to this particular mission.

Damn again.

He didn't take hits for money. He already had plenty. That's what came of gaining property during the Wars of the Roses, more of it during the Reformation years, and then constantly assuming the position of his own heir. He was financially solid. Reasonably attractive. Fit. And noble. He even wore the blue-and-silver Honor Garter just above his knee. He only accepted assassinations if there was pride, valor, and gallantry at stake. The fact that these men had taken a little six-year-old was reason enough to kill them. Wystan didn't need to challenge anyone first. He did so because it was part of his chivalric code.

And they were all failing.

Thus far.

Hmm. Perhaps they did make warriors like they used to and these bad guys just hadn't hired any. Then again, Wystan still had eight more chances. He might yet find some warriors in this gang of fourteen; someone of fighting ability…perhaps one assigned to guard a parapet. Or maybe, there would be a warrior prowling the long halls beneath the castle, the ones known for historic vaulted ceilings and massive stone construction. And, surely they'd have a warrior-type posted somewhere near the Great Hall, where puffs of intermittent smoke pointed right to their base of operation.

That wasn't too much to ask, was it?

Just one warrior?

Wystan shifted, making the slightest noise as he moved. He wore a chainmail shirt called a hauberk tonight. It reached to mid-thigh. He'd foresworn the quilted coat worn beneath the chain called a jupon. No need. Temperature wasn't an issue when one was already dead. He'd donned woolen chausses. The tights had itched when he'd been alive. And even with a ribbed knit waist, they never stayed up well. They had ties on them to attach to a jupon for that reason. He wore armored greaves to protect his lower legs, and his shoulders were protected by leather pieces called *pauldron*. Every bit of metal had been highly polished. If he had a squire, that would be the lad's job. It was an exacting task, requiring a paste of soot, water, and a hint of candle wax. It was Wystan's personal concoction. Polishing armor, and especially chainmail, took several nights. That was just getting the paste applied. Then, he'd spend another surfeit of weeks rubbing at each little link, working the paste into the metal. And then he'd buff it with the softest of suede. That way, his attire shone with every movement and in any light condition – even the silvery cast of a wintry night moon coming through any glassless oriel window he passed by.

Like tonight.

He looked a bit over-dressed and medieval, but that was to be expected. He wasn't changing to modern attire. He didn't care if he was unstylish. He'd died a knight and meant to stay one. You'd think it would make it easier to see him coming. And the last thing he'd be interested in was looking like the dead man at his feet.

This fellow wore dark trousers, a dark turtleneck sweater, and a darker-toned jacket. He blended in with the floor. And the pool of blood he was now resting in. *Hmm.* That added another dimension. The man at his feet wasn't just a lousy warrior. He was a massive bleeder, as well. Wystan moved another step back, waiting for the arterial spray to slow. No sense getting his garb dirtied.

And he'd already fed on Body Number One.

Despite any satiation, his canines grew in appreciation of the aroma. The color. The spray of droplets...getting lifted and then dispersed with the slightest of breezes. Wystan shifted to one side to avoid getting squirted with that, as well. He held his sword, tip down, and slid his blade between thumb and two fingers, watched the blood drip off it as he went.

"Halt!"

Wystan spun, the blood at the tip of his sword sent an arc of dark fluid across the stone walls, and then he grinned as a large black bulk came barreling down the corridor toward him. His assailant was backed by another fellow. Oh, good. Wystan was facing two of them.

No. Wait. A sound behind him got a head swivel and a good view of three more bodies. Ah. They were ambushing. *Excellent.* And he didn't even have to draw his sword.

Body Seven became the man at his back with the taser strike. Wystan jerked as if it had an effect just before turning his sword backwards and ramming it through the man's ribcage, where it got stuck. No worries. It gave his swing some ballast as he pulled the sword back over his head in an arc that not only pulled the taser hooks from his back but sent Body Number Seven flying toward what became Body Number Eight. Both men slammed back into the darkness, where they sent the most interesting taser-light show for a bit. Wystan didn't wait around to watch. They probably packed too much voltage in their stunners. And really. It wasn't Wystan's fault that the wires were still live when they collided. The other man who'd approached from the front had pulled his gun. Wystan retaliated by cutting his gun hand off.

Residual muscle spasms sent bullets ricocheting through the hall, adding sound and energy to an already vibrant episode. Wystan deflected more than one with his blade, sending it toward the two behind him. That was even more entertaining. Grunts followed from the two remaining men, announcing gunshot hits. Or not. Wystan didn't wait to find out. He leapt upward, did an above ground somersault, and landed behind Bodies Numbers Ten and Eleven. Number Ten got his head removed. Number Eleven took off running.

Wystan was snickering as he gave chase. Looks like chivalry was not only dead, it was buried in cowardice. He caught the fellow before he'd gone far and he didn't even use vampiric power. Wystan simply launched his sword at the fellow's legs and tripped him. Another moment and he was in front of him. Waiting for the man to stand up. He even put a hand out for an assist. Number Eleven ignored it, and slid to his feet using the rock wall.

"Do you have a sword?" Wystan asked.

"I've got something better."

"Really?"

The man drew a personal-sized sub-machine gun and pointed it at him. Wystan tipped his head slightly as if considering it.

"Ah. A fully automatic assault weapon. Impressive," he remarked finally.

"And at this range, I can't miss, Asshole."

"Well...what are you waiting for then?"

The man's finger squeezed the trigger, sending a spray of lead into the scene. He didn't live to see that none of them hit. He was impaled on Wystan's sword. And then he was sagging to a heap on the floor while Wystan pulled it back out.

"You should have asked for a sword," Wystan informed the dead body.

Number Eleven must not have used a silencer. Gunfire echoed down the hall before dying out. *Good.* Maybe that would alert the last three as to their imminent peril. And...if he guessed right, he should be closing in on the Great Hall...where they'd built their fire. And where they held their little captive. And...

Oh, damnation. Look at that. His chainmail was bloodied.

There was nothing for it. He couldn't rescue a damsel in distress if he was covered in blood. Especially a six-year-old one. Wystan unfastened his *pauldron* and shucked the hauberk, hearing it land in a puddle of chain at his feet. He refastened his shoulder protection. Damn again. He really liked that mail shirt. He made a mental note to retrieve it.

A cry came from somewhere to his left. It wasn't a frightened hurt cry. It was more the sound of sobbing. From a very young person. And it wasn't even near the Great Hall. Those bastards had placed their victim in one of Rockcliffe's towers? Without heat? Or light? That was extremely stupid of them. He wouldn't even have to mute his attack. Wystan smiled.

Oh. This was going to be pure pleasure.

The Great Hall of Rockcliffe Castle was known for its ornamental stone roof joists, the span of large, carved stone filigree openings that had once held glass, and a medieval fireplace that was intact. It had a working flue, and a rock chimney that had been reconstructed in the restoration project some Dot-Com millionaire had started at the beginning of this century, before he ran out of funds and ambition. Or both. The kidnappers must not have known that part, either. They'd piled stones into a circle, making an impromptu pit and built their fire in the center of the floor.

They were all around the fire. Silent. As if they weren't perpetrating a dastardly deed on a cold winter night. Wystan peeked around the corner of a rock-hewn doorway approximately twenty-five feet thick. He'd been right. The final three kidnappers were all there. One was wrapped in an assortment of blankets, sitting atop a stool beside the fire, and coughing occasionally. Another engrossed in drinking what appeared to be dark wine. And another was whittling away on a stick that had probably been gathered for kindling. They were all unaware and unprepared.

And maybe that wasn't so odd. Wystan had hyper-senses. Perhaps the gunfire sound from the last man hadn't been as loud as he'd thought.

"Good evening, gentlemen."

All three started and stood, mouths agape, as Wystan walked in. The stool fell. And then he was facing yet more gun barrels, held in three sets of hands.

"Just who the hell are you?" Blanket-man asked.

Wystan tipped his head in a slight bow. "Sir Wystan Ryn *de* Crecy. And don't bother with the introduction. You, of course, are the bad guys."

The drinker chuckled. "Right."

Blanket-man appeared to be their leader. He shot the drinker a glance that appeared to carry reprimand. They didn't have much discipline. The drinker smirked.

"What do you want?" Blanket-man asked.

"The girl."

"What girl?"

"The one in yon tower. So. Before we finish here and I rescue the wee damsel, I really need to know. Does any among you carry a sword?" Wystan lifted his and twisted it so firelight flicked off the blade.

"What the hell for?"

Wystan sighed heavily. "I take it that is a negative. Pity. Allow me to explain. The chivalric code being what it is, if you had carried a sword, I would have enjoined you in battle. And you might actually live a little longer."

Carving-man fired first. He'd been on Wystan's left, just inside peripheral view. His first shot went through one side of Wystan's leather *pauldron* and bit into flesh. The next five missed. That's what came of aiming while Wystan whipped around and sliced, taking not only the fellow's head off, but a good section of his shoulder and chest cavity as well. Before the body finished separating, Wystan was airborne, evading bullets as the last two men attempted to follow his movements. He landed right before the drinker, stabbed his sword into the floor in order to grab both the man's hands and twist them inward. That way, the next rounds got pumped into Drinking-man's gut and pelvic area.

The man dropped, rolled a bit, groaned. And then stilled.

But by then, Wystan was facing Blanket-man.

The fellow had run out of ammo, although he kept clicking the triggers. Wystan smacked both guns out of his hands, one after the other, using a lightning move that probably smarted. It must have, since the fellow cried out and yanked his hands to his chest.

"Any last words?" Wystan asked him.

"Are you a knight?"

"Interesting last words. Yes. I am a knight." Wystan opened his mouth wide, allowing the fellow a good look at his canines. "And I am also a vampire."

The fellow had a high-pitched scream and an affectation for dark chocolate and red wine. And a bad heart. Wystan got little more than a taste before the fellow's heart stopped beating and the body slumped into lifelessness. It was just as well. Now that he'd slain the dragons, he had a tower to gird, and a damsel to rescue.

And look. He even had a blanket to use.

The Carlotti grand-daughter was a lovely girl. She was dressed as a princess, ethereal-looking in a pink dress with a full tulle skirt. She had a little tiara atop her curls. Wystan stopped momentarily, sitting astride the tower window ledge to fully appreciate her. He'd rescued many damsels. None had actually looked the part. He couldn't prevent the smile. And then she addressed him, and changed everything.

"Who are you?"

"I am your rescuer."

"Really?"

"Are you cold?"

Wystan stepped into the room, proffering the blankets with one hand, and using the other to adjust the grommets holding his shoulder *pauldron* in place, before moving them to the waist of his chausses to hitch them up. He hadn't considered how immodest he might look. Maybe he should have used the blanket like a cloak. A moment later he was sure of it.

"You're very handsome," she informed him.

"Uh…"

"Are you a knight?"

"Sir Wystan Ryn *de* Crecy. At your service, miss." Wystan performed a courtly bow, and then had to hitch his chausses up again. Damn things.

"Are you married?"

"Uh…" Wystan's brows rose. He didn't know how to answer that. She was truly lovely. Cute. Precocious.

"I think I want to marry you."

She'd reached him. Her head was level with his waist. She had a mass of curly dark hair, and the fake jewels on her tiara twinkled in the light. Wystan caught the smile.

"I think…you're a mite young yet, miss."

"I won't always be. Will you wait for me?"

CHAPTER TWO

Uh oh.

She was looking up at him. Moonlight touched cherubic cheeks, the shadow of lashes, and an expression akin to the one most women gave him within moments of seeing him. Good thing he had cell phones back at the helicopter. And VAL Headquarters on speed-dial.

"Can we speak of such things later, *demoiselle*? We need to complete your rescue first. For that, we're going to do a bit of a jump."

"You can jump from here?"

She was at the window opening, looking down approximately four stories. Good thing she was young. And might not remember such things. She turned her head to look back up to him.

"Will you have to hold me?" she asked next.

"Pretty much," Wystan answered. And then he shifted to another leg.

"Will that make us engaged?"

Wystan looked heavenward for a moment. At least they'd put her in a tower with an intact roof.

He could see the wood vaulting. And remnants of a bird nest. She sounded serious. But she couldn't be. She was so very young. And so very cute. Perhaps she was play-acting with him, using her role of princess. And he could just play along.

He looked back down and gave her another bow. And then had to hitch his chausses up again. Now was not a good time to rue the fact that he'd foregone the jupon. It still happened.

"I am but a poor knight, m'lady. You should truly hold out for a prince."

"But once you marry me, you'd be a prince."

That was just his luck. She had temerity, looked pretty darling, and wasn't lacking in wits. Wystan decided on another tack. Adventure. Excitement. He elevated his voice to show it.

"You ever ride in a helicopter, Miss Carlotti?"

"Lots of times. Why?"

Well. That killed the adventurous, exciting part of it. "Because we've got a Euro-copter awaiting us."

"You don't have a horse?"

Wystan chuckled before he could prevent it. And then he shook his head ruefully. "Sadly…no. Apologies."

"I'll buy you one."

"Ah. My thanks. But I do already have one. He's…a bit under the weather at the moment."

…and six feet of earth.

"My daddy is very rich."

This was getting problematical. Wystan didn't deal with women or problems very well. And nobody had said a word about just how precocious Miss Carlotti could be. He had her wrapped securely in a blanket and tucked beneath his arm before she said another word. And then they swooped out the window.

Moments later he was bent over, ignoring how his chausses sagged, displaying a good section of his lower back to the night air, in order to deposit his bundle in a back seat. He strapped her in. And then he opened the top of the blanket, making sure she'd survived the journey. Dark eyes, set in spectacular lashes surveyed him for a moment before she smiled.

Buggers.

His situation had not improved. Wystan turned toward the pilot. VAL had assigned Vaughn for this hit. The fellow was their best. Or so he claimed. He'd also had a recent run-in with some sort of finger ripping apparatus. Wystan had noticed the fake skin on most of his fingertips when they'd met. It didn't hamper his flying skill. Vaughn gave him a salute from the pilot seat. Wystan frowned.

"Looks like everything went okay. And in less than twenty minutes. Wow. You guys never fail to amaze. I didn't have time to finish my coffee."

"Fire it up. You've got a rendezvous with some very concerned parents."

"Take a seat and strap in first. Oh. Never mind. You're a vampire. Do whatever you want."

The engine started up. A tremor went through the enclosure. The blades started rotating, sending more air onto his backside. Good thing he was immune from tactile sensation. He couldn't conquer the flush, however.

"Can you handle Miss Carlotti?" Wystan turned his head to ask.

"Solo? Oh, hell no. Get in. Your ticket is for two tonight."

Damn.

Wystan pulled his chausses to his waist, slid into his seat, and closed the door. Then he fished a slim-phone from the seat pocket before him. He didn't strap in. He might need to bail. He pressed the button with the "6" on it. He didn't have to press the "call" button. These phones were coded just for him. Good thing. Wystan wasn't a fan of technology.

"VAL Headquarters. Nigel speaking. Who's calling please?"

"Is Akron in?"

"Oh. Hi there, Sir Galahad. Nice of you to check in."

"Akron?"

"Geez. Not one of you assassins has a bent toward small talk. Exchanging witty repartee. I'm telling you, it's a wasted art. Completely wasted. Hold your pants up, bud. I'm connecting you."

Wystan pulled the phone from his ear and stared at it. It was just Nigel's terminology, but it was too accurate by far. But loose tights were the least of his troubles. Akron's voice came through the phone next.

"*De* Crecy? You there?"

"Sir!" Wystan fumbled with the phone.

"So. Speak up."

"I have a small problem."

"Checking. Nothing reportable from Cornwall this evening. Nothing from Rockcliffe Castle. Nothing about murder and mayhem. Actually…there's nothing newsworthy coming in from anywhere on the coast. I suppose you left a mess. Is that it?"

"Well...there were fourteen of them. And they were armed."

"So be it. I'll send a 4D Team. Send the Yellow one, Nigel. They have the most finesse. Ownership of Rockcliffe Castle might be in dispute, and it's already a ruin...but I rather like it."

"That's not why I called."

"Really?"

"It's...Miss Carlotti."

"She's safe?"

Odd. Akron made it sound as if the answer better be affirmative or someone was perishing. And doing it in a horrid fashion.

"Of course. She's right beside me. Bundled in blankets. Strapped into a seat. About forty minutes from touch-down."

"And this is a problem?"

"It's not that kind of problem."

"This should be good. Nigel? You listening?"

"Oh, please sir. As if I'd forego hearing this. Of course I'm listening."

"You have eight seconds left, *de* Crecy. Want to call back?"

Wystan slapped the phone closed against his thigh. He toyed with pitching it out the window before placing it back in the seat pocket.

"Are you...in trouble?"

Miss Carlotti asked it from beside him. Wystan slid a glance toward her. She'd intersected her query with a yawn. That was even cute. She was the epitome of cute. Why...if cuteness had a ranking of one to ten, she was a twelve.

"Not really," he replied.

"Oh. Good."

She just sat there, regarding him with sleepy eyes. If he was really lucky, she might go to sleep. And then she woke she'd be in the arms of her loving family, and all of this would be a forgotten.

Maybe.

What was he thinking? He wasn't that lucky.

He pulled out another phone, pressed "6" again, and turned slightly, putting a shoulder toward her. All the phones assigned to him tonight were set to the same number. This time it didn't even ring before Akron was talking.

"Well, Nigel? What did they say? Excellent. Oh. Hello again, *de* Crecy. We just sent the alert to Miss Carlotti's parents. Needless to say, they're thrilled. They can't wait to meet you and thank you in person."

"Not a good plan, sir. I need to disappear. Fade from memory, if you wish. Vaughn can take the credit."

"Just what is going on over there?"

"It's Miss Carlotti. She, uh…she wants to marry me."

Nigel started laughing first. It echoed through the speaker. Wystan was frowning before Akron's booming laugh came through, loud enough it drowned out the sound of the rotating blades.

"It's not funny," Wystan informed them when he could be heard again.

"Forgive us, *de* Crecy. I thought it was something serious."

"It *is* serious."

"Since this happens every time you get spotted, I would think you'd be used to it. Or, have a game plan in place."

"Or maybe, ask for an assist," Nigel added.

"Like from me."

"She's six years old," Wystan informed them.

"She'll grow."

"Yes. I know. She has already informed me of that fact," Wystan replied.

Both men chuckled again. Wystan set his jaw and waited.

"You know, you might wish to consider toning down some of the valiant knight routine. It might make you a little less appealing."

"I'd like some more immediate help, sir."

"Very well, *de* Crecy. Bail before you land. I'll alert Vaughn to his new role as hero. What is it now, Nigel?"

Wystan couldn't hear what Nigel said. All he heard was Akron's reply.

"Not good enough. Lizbeth is not trained. Yes, Wystan *de* Crecy has always had women trouble. No. I don't think it will rub off."

Wystan ended the call. They called it women trouble? He called it a nuisance, and a big one at that. All he wanted was—

Damn everything!

He'd forgotten his hauberk back at Rockcliffe. His shoulders sagged slightly. He supposed he could divert back and fetch it. It was out of the way. His estate was in the borderlands between England and Wales, the area called the *Marche*. Returning for his chain would cost hours and he'd just lost three of them. He'd planned on drafting the helicopter for the ride to his home. That was out. He'd have to take a car.

The helicopter started its descent. A glance showed Miss Carlotti asleep beside him. She was even cuter in that mode, he decided. A glance the other direction showed all kinds of lights. He could see a mass of people below. Journalist type people. With cameras. Wystan jerked the handle of the door open and slid out. He refastened the door, and then dropped out of sight. Vaughn hadn't even noticed.

He didn't need the hauberk. He had others. Historians could have a field day with it when the crime unit released it. All he needed was to be home. He could almost feel the solitude. The solid stone slab he rested atop. Sense the aura of quietude away from bothersome females and the complications that ensued from any contact. He wanted his crypt.

It seemed hours later when he finally closed in on it.

Wystan stopped for a bit at one side of his gatehouse. Had he any animation, his chest would have swelled with pride. The entire Crecy estate was on display in the silvered moonlight. It was magnificent. Orderly. Structured. Registered in any number of history books. But it was earlier than he'd projected. It didn't appear to be much past midnight. He supposed he could draft his driver into one more trip...

And just then, the strangest rumble came through the air, lifting strands of his hair and brushing across his exposed skin.

Oh. Bother.

He'd forgotten. He'd agreed to host a Winter Renaissance Faire. An elderly woman had cornered him in his study several months ago. It had been a dark, dreary day. She'd found him awake and restless. She'd asserted her way into his presence. Hounded him. She wouldn't take no for an answer. And she'd shown way too much leg for his taste. He'd agreed to allow a Faire on the parade grounds of Crecy Castle mainly to get rid of her. He'd been afraid to continue the conversation.

A knee-high carpet of mist rose from the ground, enveloping his lower legs. It wet the armor of his shin guards and dampened his chausses to mid-thigh. That's what came of a night with a full moon and higher-than-normal temperatures. Wystan skimmed the ground, skirting the outer wall, sticking to shadows, avoiding detection. He went the long way around, avoiding the parade grounds where they'd set up their tents. The graveyard was on the opposite end of the bailey. It would be deserted, as always. Nobody ever went there.

Another wave of air assailed him, this time knocking him off his feet. He flew several feet before slamming against the stone of his barbican wall.

What the hell?

Wystan spun, sword already pulled, and head lowered. There wasn't anyone in sight. No Hunters. Nothing. But something was odd. Something in the air. A scent. A feeling. An awakening. And he actually felt a chill.

He *felt* it!

His eyes went wide as he looked down, watching real gooseflesh form on his chest and lower belly.

He could feel temperature? Oh, sweet prophecy! If what he suspected was true, he was the luckiest dead man in existence. He grasped his sword handle tighter and actually felt the metal hilt warping against his fingers. It was true! All of it. Everything he'd been told.

He had a mate.

She was in his sphere.

All he had to do was find her.

He hitched up his now thoroughly-dampened chausses and straightened his *pauldron*. And then he was stalking across the lists, intent on attending the Crecy Castle Winter Renaissance Faire. He didn't think to change into more modest apparel. He didn't ponder consequences. He had a mate. She was in that mass of people somewhere. And he had to find her.

Thank goodness that old lady had talked him into this.

CHAPTER THREE

"Twelve forty a.m. Ten minutes late. You don't think he got spooked, do you?"

Rachel Berne returned to scanning the crowd. Her target had looked to be in the forty to forty-five age range. Executive-looking. Dark haired with a receding hairline. Silver-tipped temples. Dark eyed.

And he had a taste for pedophilia.

It wasn't much to go on, and was probably false. Just like her on-line identity as Jamie, a nine-year-old boy who'd just escaped from another horrible foster home. Her pedophile had sent a fuzzy picture last week – before she found out he was in England. Well. Wherever he was hiding, she was finding him. She didn't care how far she had to go. She'd spent too much time on this guy to let him wriggle away.

Besides, Britain was only a plane flight away. And…according to the psychologist report, she needed a vacation from chasing this particular sexual predator, anyway. Nobody seemed to notice that her ex-partner and friend, Eleanor Munson, took on the assignment in Rachel's place. Hell. Nobody had even asked.

Hmm...

According to the pedophile's picture, he was in good shape. Fairly nice looking. He claimed to be six foot in height. Three inches taller than her. He should be easy to spot. *If* he hadn't been yanking her chain with a dummy description. But even if he'd given her a hook, line, and sinker with his online personae, one thing was certain. He would be searching the crowd, too. Unlike her, however, he'd probably be more comfortably dressed.

Rachel didn't know anything about Renaissance Faire attire, but there seemed to be a lot of breast flesh on display. Much more than necessary – but that also included her. That's what happened when she crammed her Double D's into a tight square bodice, and then slapped on a ribcage-smashing corset as outerwear. It also meant she had to keep her weapons in her skirt pockets or on a thigh. Her cuffs were in a pocket. The pocketknife was in another. The taser was in a thigh holster. She'd have to reach through the hole she'd cut in one skirt pocket to get to it. That would cost precious seconds. Good thing she was a third-degree black belt in Karate. A stunner would be the least of the perp's problems.

She'd rather have a bra-holster like usual. She'd also like to have her Walther PPK. But, no. Not this trip. This was the UK. No guns. And she wasn't even supposed to here. Besides, this bodice was barely large enough for her bosom. She yanked a bit on the ruffle edge framing her cleavage, and then moved to rearrange her sleeve back over her wristwatch. She did it without looking.

"Damn it, Berne. We were told. Authentic attire."

"Oh. Please." Rachel tilted her head toward her companion then had to push a mass of gauze off her shoulder so it could return to trailing down her back. That amount of material was just nonsense, as was the cone atop her head where the veil was hooked. The headdress was called a *hennin.* It made her top-heavy and ungainly if she moved too quickly. She didn't have to guess. She knew. The one time she'd tried to turn around normally, she'd almost toppled over, much to the amusement of everyone in the vicinity at the time. "I'm wearing a corset, five hundred yards of material, really tight ankle boots that button, something skimpy called a chemise…and you're complaining about a wristwatch?"

"Yes."

"Too bad. I need it."

"You want the time, I'll check in with the guys."

"Not on your life. They're still whistling and making jokes over my outfit. Jerks. It must be a male thing: How to be a jerk. Instructions granted upon birth. Even back in the middle ages."

"I'm not following you."

"Would a woman have designed this attire? Honest opinion, Munson. If a woman was involved, would she truly design tons and tons of skirt and no underwear? Come on. We both know she'd have crafted a panties and a bra."

"Oh. They had bras. I read about it. One was just discovered in a castle…I think in Austria. It had been wadded into a wall for insulation or something. Sixteenth century. Seventeenth, maybe. I didn't pay that much attention."

"Why the hell didn't you say so?"

"It wouldn't help you, Berne. Sorry. It didn't have underwire. Besides, I think it's a small cup. Not your size. And before you bitch some more, let me say, I'm envious. I'd guess half the women here are having the same issue."

Rachel ignored most of that. There was a six foot tall man to her right. Thirties. He was dressed as a musketeer with a wig and mustache combo that screamed fakery. He wasn't searching for much. He appeared to be very happy chatting up two female, steam-punk aficionados, neither of whom looked much under her age. Rachel checked her watch again.

Beside her, Officer Eleanor Munson cleared her throat. Rachel looked back down at her.

"Give it a rest, okay? It's a wristwatch. I've seen more than a dozen cell phones. Not all of this lighting is fire-based, and that last vendor even had an electric heater going in his tent."

"How do you know?"

"It was warm."

"He was hawking leather goods. They might keep it warm."

"He also had an extension cord tucked along the tent edge. Or perhaps you didn't notice. And…will you look there? If my senses do not deceive, that is a coffee stand."

"Where?"

"Just beyond the black striped tent. Hard to miss. Can't you hear that espresso machine?"   Rachel snickered. "Real authentic, medieval stuff, there. You want a latte? I'll buy."

"Maybe we should go back to the mead hall."

"We arranged to meet near the south entrance." Rachel checked her watch again. Twelve forty-five. He was fifteen minutes late. But maybe the perp didn't know his compass directions. There were two other entrances. All being watched. She turned around in a large circular fashion. Beside her, Munson followed suit.

"Where are we going?"

"Nowhere. We're strolling. Chatting with folks. Trying to look authentic. You know, doing medieval woman stuff. Oh, hey. Look at this get-up. I didn't think they had spandex tights and thigh-high, hooker boots back then. I'm going to take a pass on whether or not they wore peplum jackets in green satin with black bows. They probably had those."

"What? Where?"

"Two o'clock and heading this way. Oh. Wait. That's a guy."

"Oh. No. That is... It's—."

"Oh. Allow me to finish. It's wrong on so many levels there are no words. We're going to need eye bleach. And crap. He's coming right for us."

"Ah. Ladies. Good evening to you both."

Hooker Boots stopped in front of them and did what was probably a bow. It looked silly. Especially with the lean legs he'd put on display in skin-tight black tights. He also sported a large codpiece thing atop his genitals that was in the same green satin as his jacket. He wasn't paying the least attention to Eleanor. Or Rachel. He was pretty much focused right on the Double Ds that he'd addressed as 'ladies'. Why…if they weren't chasing a pedophile, Rachel would have slapped her cuffs on him just for that look.

"Good eve to you, kind sir."

Officer Munson curtsied and tapped his arm with her fan, trying to gain attention. It wasn't working. Eleanor was a Special Investigator assigned to the PP & SS division, as was Rachel. Tracking down Predatory Pedophiles and prosecuting Sexual Slavers was the mission. Eleanor was good at her job. Unfortunately, she wasn't endowed with much bosom, and she was barely shoulder height on Rachel. She had been blessed with spectacular legs, however. She'd gone undercover as a dancer/stripper before and pulled it off. Not tonight. Apparently, great legs were not a feature they cared about in the Middle Ages.

And right then, Rachel saw him.

Forty five, my ass.

A man emerged from between the shadow cast by two tents: one, a smoked turkey-leg vendor doing a brisk business, the other, a seller of beaded paraphernalia who looked bored. Rachel narrowed her eyes. The potential target looked about mid-twenties. Five-six maybe. Pudgy, if the amount of chin was any indicator. He was dressed in black and orange, diamond-patterned pants and a matching jacket. She'd have ignored him if he hadn't been engrossed in scanning the area. He wasn't looking for anyone tall, either. His gaze was checking for little people.

Young, little people.

Good thing. He'd have caught her studying him.

He had a vague resemblance to the photo on file, although she couldn't tell hair color and baldness through his joker hat with three pointy things that actually appeared to have bells at the ends. From general appearance, it looked like he hadn't sent a stranger's photo to her. He'd sent one of his father.

"And your companion? The oh-so-luscious lady?"

"Luscious?"

Eleanor answered. Good thing. Hooker Boots demonstrated meaning by performing the universal sign for large tits with his hands before his chest. If Rachel had been involved in the conversation, she'd have seriously considered shock treatment. Electrifying Hooker Boots with a taser actually sounded like a viable option. Except she'd lose track of her man.

And hell. With her luck, the crew stationed at the back of the admittance tent was filming this.

"Oh, honey. I'm sorry. We're going to be busy." Eleanor told him.

"How about tomorrow evening?"

"Busy."

"The day after?"

"Yes. Busy then, too."

"Both of you?"

"Well. Yes. We'll always be busy. That's what happens with lesbians, honey."

Rachel snorted and turned her head back slightly…just enough that she could still watch the joker between the tents, and pretend to pay attention to Eleanor as she lopped an arm about Rachel's waist.

"Oh, really?"

Shit. If anything, Hooker Boots sounded even more intrigued. His next words proved it.

"You wouldn't consider a *ménage-a-trois*, would you?"

Eleanor laughed. It didn't sound amused. Rachel caught her tongue between her teeth and stuck her chin forward. Oh. Cuffs and electric shock were too good. What Hooker Boots really needed was a Karate back-knuckle blow. That might teach him some manners.

Wait. Their potential pedophile had moved back, encasing his body again in shadow. He was still there, however. Torchlight was glinting off one of his hat bells.

"Beat it, buddy. Okay?" Eleanor had completely lost any humor. Hooker Boots didn't seem to catch it.

"Is that a no?"

"It's a no, and then it's punctuated with a *hell* no. You need to move on before I get annoyed. Got it?"

He must've understood. Rachel didn't move her head to check. She took a step toward the bead-seller's tent, surreptitiously keeping an eye on the tell-tale glint of joker's bells.

"Can you believe the nerve of—oh! Baby. Abs."

"What?" Rachel asked.

"Abs. Abs. Holy shit. I am looking at abs to die for. Are you blind?"

"Could you stop man-watching for half a second?"

Rachel took another slow, measured step toward the court jester's hiding spot. This was workable. She could pretend to look toward the beaded ware, while keeping their man in line of sight. Eleanor didn't make the same move. Her arm tightened around Rachel's waist.

"Rachel? Seriously. Rachel?"

"You want me to—?"

Rachel's words stopped. Her jaw dropped. Literally. Her view got completely cut off by six-foot-five of absolute god. And somebody looked like he'd gotten the attire right. The man who'd blocked her was dressed in low slung dark trousers that didn't do much to hide anything, leather shoulder things that just made him look broader, armored shin guards on his lower legs, and a sword that looked not only authentic, but pretty deadly, as well. Munson hadn't been fibbing about his physique, either. His abs were truly amazing. That was before she factored in his pecs. Arms. And an upward look got her a view of a face that stole what breath she'd gained.

Rachel's eyes went wide. It felt like someone had sucker punched her. Her breasts got a massive dose of tingling. For the first time she appreciated exactly why nobody wore a bra back then, even if they could have. The sensation of real linen as it rubbed against her nipples transferred all the way through her. It even weakened her knees so that she wobbled momentarily before catching it.

Tall, dark, and handsome was a cliché. And it wasn't remotely accurate. There was handsome, and then there was holy shit gorgeous. And then he added to the effect by stabbing the tip of his sword into the ground at the edge of her skirt, and going to a knee. That position, one knee raised, and both hands about the sword hilt, gave her a fantastic view of massive shoulders and arms, muscular pecs, and jaw-dropping abs. Rachel put a hand to her bosom to hold back the sigh. That even felt right.

She probably looked exactly like a model for a renaissance painting.

His head was just above waist-level. Receding hair was not an issue. He had a full head of gorgeous hair. And then he looked up and caught her in a rapt gaze. Buzzing filled her ears, as if someone had tased her or something. Eyes the same shade as his hair locked with hers for heart-stopping moments.

She'd never felt like this.

She'd never seen such depth.

His eyes were magnetic. Enthralling. Hypnotic. She forgot everything about her purpose. The assignment. Everything. And then he spoke, putting such an amazing depth of voice into the area, the entire world seemed to stop and listen.

"My lady. I have found you. Finally."

Oh. Holy shit was not even close.

"You might as well give up, man. She's a lesbian!"

Hooker Boots called it from somewhere. And before Rachel could rebut it, the clear and distinct sound of a cry split the area – a young, nine-year-old- boy sound of cry.

CHAPTER FOUR

"My name's not Jamie! Help!"

Whatever spell had been cast, the cry for help broke it. Rachel moved instantly, hiking her skirts up with one hand, and grabbing at her *hennin* with the other. She took off for the shadowy area. There was a boy standing there, wrapped in the arms of a woman – presumably his mother – Rachel wasn't stopping. Munson could find out details, because the area was now empty of their man.

Shit.

Rachel sprinted between the tents, emerging into the shadow-land separating one row of vendor tents from the next. Back here, it was a different world. And it wasn't well-lit. The tents didn't have the bright stripes on their back sides. They all looked to be dull and dark. The nearest exit was on her left. She almost went that way. A flash of orange and black patterned attire caught her eyes, sending her the other direction. He was avoiding the closest escape? That was short-sighted and stupid of him. Munson had probably already sent the signal, and every exit was already blocked by police.

Then again, they wouldn't know they were chasing a chubby court jester.

And he was winning. The skirts were getting soggy. That made them heavier. Unwieldy. She was ready to rip the cone off her head and to hell with the hair she might lose, and the corset about her waist was crippling. And then she tripped over a tent line.

She didn't fall far.

The gorgeous guy who'd been worshipping at her feet caught her about the waist and the next moment she was wrapped in an arm, held against his side. The other hand held that sword. And double holy shit. She hadn't even seen him move. They were still moving as well – with a speed that meshed the wall of tents into one long blur.

"Who are we chasing?" he asked at her ear.

"Joker. Orange…and black…outfit."

She sounded incoherent to her own ears. It wasn't her fault. If she had access to breath, she'd have made sense. He looked up, craning his neck, and then he nodded. Rachel was set on her feet with a jolt and leaned against a utility, wire-bearing light pole. Who the hell puts a light pole in the back alley of a renaissance faire? And why the hell couldn't they have seen the lights at the top illuminated? Probably wouldn't match the authenticity rule. She barely had time to grab it for stability before Sir Gorgeous was gone. A blink of time later she heard a distinct cry of pain coming from the murky area at least three tents beyond her.

"Wait! Don't kill him!"

Rachel was on the move again, not even questioning why such a warning would be necessary. She just knew. And when she finally rounded the last tent, it was more than obvious, even in what light hit the scene. Sir Gorgeous was dangling Joker-Guy by one leg, his big-ass sword was aimed for the perp's bowel-area, and that fellow was blubbering something about mercy.

"Mercy! Please! Don't kill me! Mercy!"

Rachel parroted the words, although hers came in a breathless, 'come-hither' voice she didn't know she owned. It was the corset's fault. Damn thing. Even if they were sexier than hell, she wasn't wearing one again. She was out of breath, and had a painful stitch in her left side. She shoved a hand there and pressed, while the other fished in a pocket for her cuffs.

"Don't kill...him," she repeated.

Sir Gorgeous looked across at her and lifted the perp about a foot higher. "You want him alive?"

"Not...really."

The sword moved, flashing a pinprick of light from some source beyond the moonlit alley. Screw the cuffs. Rachel threw herself at Sir Gorgeous' sword arm, and held on. The stitch in her side sent an arc of fire through her, and even that didn't cancel out how direct contact with this man felt. *Wow.* Her fingers wrapped about his upper arm as if she wanted to caress an excellent example of a sculpted bicep.

"Don't...kill him," she whispered.

"You tell him, lady!"

"Shut up," Rachel looked at the perp before returning to his captor. "Look. You need...to put him down. Okay?"

"Now?"

"Well…soon. I've got…to cuff…him. Get…somebody…to read his rights. Or whatever legalities…are required in this shire."

She still sounded like she was whispering sexually charged words. No wonder he acted like he didn't understand. He simply stood there, holding up approximately two hundred pounds of struggling human, while gazing at her with those bottomless dark eyes. Rachel was snagged. And from somewhere in her auditory range, buzzing started up again. She barely managed to escape the weird sense of enthrallment by turning her head, averting her gaze to a tent beside her. She removed her hands next, one after the other. Her fingers were even tingling. She'd never felt such an overwhelming sense of alertness.

She had to step back. Get some space between them. Find her wits. Get her libido back where it belonged: under her control. Rachel put her hand against her side again and leaned into it. The corset actually gapped a bit at the pressure. She couldn't get a deep breath, but it was better than before. She bought more time by licking her lips.

"Well, you heard the lady. Release me."

The perp moved upward with a quick motion. A moment later he was in a heap on the ground. Immobile. Rachel's mouth went as wide as her eyes.

"You…killed him?"

Damn everything. She didn't sound appalled and shocked. Her statement was more in the breathless and excited range.

"No."

He sheathed his sword into a scabbard at his back. She knew what was happening because the vague image of his shadow on the ground. She didn't watch. She didn't dare see all that muscle in action. She was actually afraid to look up at him again.

"Look. Thanks, Mister…uh. I don't even know your name."

Her words were jumbled and her hands didn't work properly. She stuck them in her pockets, and didn't bring out cuffs. She'd fished out her taser from her thigh holster. Rachel moved it back and forth in her hand, wondering why nothing was making sense.

Why stun.

It sounded like he'd said something. She looked down at the weapon she held. Oh. Their guy was already out. No wonder he asked.

"Because I didn't bring my gun, okay?"

She dared a glance upward. His brows were drawn together in a semi-frown. That look caused a tremor throughout her back, down her legs, and it seemed to even make it through the tight ankle boots. Holy shit! She'd never come up against such solid sex appeal. In one package. She returned to looking at the taser in her hand.

"I do not understand your reply," he answered.

"Look. I'm not from around here. I'm from New York. I'm here, uh…helping with an assignment. And I don't piss in somebody else's pool." And she was getting her breath back. Nice.

It took some time before he answered. She had plenty of time to look over her stun gun. Trigger. Electrical wiring.

"I do not understand that, either."

"You asked why I stun people. I'm answering. I don't act as judge, jury, and executioner. That's somebody else's department. I only arrest them and move on. As far as I know, this is an alleged sexual predator, and I'm putting the emphasis on *alleged,* got it?"

He moved closer, blocking out every bit of light. And then his index finger went beneath her chin and lifted her to face him again. And oh shit. Her knees actually wobbled.

"You misunderstood. I gave you my name. Wystan."

Okay. She had to be hearing it wrong. She could blame the buzzing that had restarted the longer she locked eyes with him. Who named their kids such weird-ass names? Then again, what did she know? This was Britain. That name might be perfectly normal.

"Why-stun?"

"Yes. Wystan Ryn *de* Crecy."

He let go of her chin and stepped back in order to execute a slight bow. It probably resembled the one Hooker Boots had done, but it looked a hell of a lot sexier. That was probably due to those low-slung pant-things he was wearing, and that spectacular physique. And she really had to get her mouth moving. Rachel cleared her throat.

"Okay. Wystan. Well. I'm Rachel. Rachel Berne. And…I'm going to do you a favor. Something completely against protocol."

"What is it?"

"Disappear. Now."

"Disappear?"

"Unless you like police procedure. Paperwork. Questioning. Lots of long hours in a cold room. That kind of thing."

"Is that where you are going?"

Oh...sweet. That sounded like he might be interested. Maybe not as much as her, but things could be worse. Rachel couldn't believe she was thinking along this line. One should not hook-up over the body of an unconscious perpetrator. It just didn't feel right. She shoved the taser into a pocket and searched about for cuffs. And got nothing. How the hell could she have dropped them?

"I...don't have firm plans, actually," she finally replied.

"Ah. Good. You are free."

"Look. Maybe you could just give me your number. I'll call you."

"I do not have a number."

"You don't have a cell?" *Or...maybe you are just saying no?*

"No."

Well. That proved it. He was saying no. Rachel's belly actually fell at the rejection. And the guy at their feet punctuated the surreal scene by groaning and doing a slight roll.

"You need to secure him," Sir Gorgeous pointed out.

"Yeah. I know. But...I sort of lost my cuffs." *Geez.* If the London guys at the attendance booth found out, they'd never cease teasing her over it, too.

"Then, I will stay."

"Berne! You in there somewhere?"

Eleanor's floated through the alley, sounding like she was about two tents away. Wystan turned his head toward the sound.

"Ah. The other woman arrives. She will have the means to secure him?"

"No doubt."

"Then I shall leave you, most fair lady. But not for long."

He lifted her hand and touched a kiss to her knuckles and disappeared. There was no other word for it. One moment she was looking at six-foot-five male, and the next there was just dark empty space. And then there was Eleanor Munson's face.

And sanity.

CHAPTER FIVE

"You've reached VAL Headquarters…where death really does come at a price. Ours. Nigel speaking. How may I direct your call?"

"Is Akron in?"

"Oh. Look. It's Sir Galahad again. Let me guess. You need another rescue. More women are chasing you down."

"Don't call me that."

"Hey. I just read a book on Arthurian legend, and quite frankly, you should be flattered. Galahad was their purest knight. The most noble. The most—"

"Galahad was celibate, Nigel," Akron's voice interrupted.

"Exactly! Celibate. Just like—oh, crap! It's you, sir. Ahem. I was just about to contact you. *De* Crecy is on the line again."

"And his business is…?"

"I was just about to ask. *De* Crecy? Why are you calling, please?"

"I need a number."

"Oh. Allow me, please. How about eight," Nigel answered.

"Nigel."

The speakers resounded with Akron's voice. It rattled two of the statues in Wystan's crypt. It also echoed for some moments before the sound dulled to a slight humming noise.

"What? He wanted a number. I gave him one."

"You're a bit testy this evening. Issues?"

"Oh. It's nothing. Nothing really. Can we just move on?"

"You haven't been betting with Lizbeth again, have you? Still attempting to prove male superiority?"

"She said she could get a higher score than me on VIDWAR because she can use the algorithms behind the game plays. She knows which hits gain more points and goes after them. She said it doesn't matter how many times a player dies and re-spawns. What matters is getting the right kills in the shortest amount of time."

"Ah. Dexterity versus strategy. I see. And you lost?"

"So now I have to watch her play *my* game on *my* monitor while I research the Knights of the Round Table. It's not funny."

Akron was definitely chuckling. It didn't last.

"Forgive me, Nigel. I just find you so...refreshingly young. Perhaps we should get back to Sir Wystan's call, before he runs out of time?"

"Oh. Sir Galahad? Grab a new phone. We'll call you right back."

The cell in Wystan's hand went dead. That matched most of the surroundings. The Crecy family crypt was constructed of gray stone. It had a huge sculpted angel on the roof peak outside. Inside, the designers had carried over the same scheme. Reliefs of fallen angels were carved along every wall, their arms reaching as if to embrace a niche containing a shrouded skeleton. The four stone pedestals in the floor had the same imagery. Carved angel wings supported stone slabs for holding the same type of occupant. Shrouded. Still. Skeletal. Dead.

One was empty.

His.

Wystan wasn't in here to rest. He'd had to leave his mate's proximity or react. And this was where he kept his bin full of cell phones. One of them vibrated before a low tone emitted from to it. Wystan fished it out, pushed the "call" button, pressed it to his ear, and started pacing again.

"All right, *de* Crecy. I do have to agree with Nigel. It's a woman. That being the case, I already started a search. I see you are in the middle of a weekend Winter Renaissance Faire…on your castle grounds."

"Yes, I know."

"Well, for a recluse, that behavior is rather odd. What time is it over there? Two in the morning?"

"Yes."

"You expect this faire to go all night?"

"I don't know."

"Well, I do know. It's in the fine print of the contract that you signed. Ah. Look here. They will shut down operations between the hours of four a.m. and eight. Just long enough to sober up, I assume. That was generous of you. What on earth made you agree to this?"

"I just need a cell number, sir."

"That is a negative."

Wystan stopped walking. He stared at one of his dead ancestors.

"We don't put traceable technology in the hands of a novice. At least, not until someone offers up particulars. You have found your mate. Yes?"

"No way," Nigel inserted. "He did *not* have that happen. We just talked to him this afternoon. Four hours ago. Max. No. I don't believe it. No."

"We'll need particulars, Wystan. Where is she?" Akron asked.

"How do we know she's not with him?" Nigel asked.

"He's requesting a cell phone number, Nigel."

"Oh. Yeah. Right. So, tell us already, Galahad. Where is your mate? And I hope she's old and ugly and shriveled-up and—"

"Nigel. Do you want me to intercede with Lizbeth?"

"Oh, no sir. That would be tantamount to surrender."

"Very good. Then keep to the job at hand. Before we need another connection."

"What was it again?"

"Sir Wystan's mate. And her location. And you can speak at any time, *de* Crecy. It might save Nigel."

"Oh. She's in some cold room. Doing something about police procedure."

"Your mate is in law enforcement? Hmm. That could get a bit…complicated. Especially when you consider our line of work. Nigel. Start searching for police activity in the *Marshe* area. Nothing? Use the

Abyss Link. Look for hidden activity. Covert. Special operations. Ah. Here it is. Apparently there was a sting operation at your estate tonight. It involved a nasty sexual predator. A female officer from the states is being credited with the collar, despite the perpetrator's words of a giant fellow with a large sword. That's rather interesting."

"I can explain," Wystan replied.

"Later, maybe. At the moment, I need to know the name of your mate. It could get a lot more complicated if it's Eleanor Munson."

"No. She said her name was Rachel. Rachel Berne."

"Got her. Screen image coming up...now, and...well."

"Wow! She's just...*wow*."

Nigel punctuated his words with a low whistle. Wystan's eyes narrowed on the wall as he fought the rise of something he hadn't felt in centuries. Could it be emotion? He was feeling anger? Jealousy?

"Well. That decides that. We can't issue you a number. Nor, can we give you hers."

"Why not?"

"Law enforcement personnel are not fond of things like searching unauthorized data bases and phone tampering. Not only that, but it amounts to what humans have titled the crime of stalking. Trust me on this."

"How can I contact her, then?"

"Let me think. Does she have any special interests that you know of?"

"Maybe. What's a lesbian?"

Nigel choked and then was sputtering all kinds of words. "Oh, man! You gotta be kidding me! Can I tell him, sir? Can I? Please? Let me do it. Please? Oh, please?"

"Go ahead, Nigel. I'll do research. And this, I've got to hear. Oh. Keep it clean. You're speaking to a knight of the Honor Order here, not one of your Seventies peers."

"Clean? Okay. Here goes. Sir Galahad! Buddy! You are either the most curst vampire in history…or the luckiest undead man walking. I'll start with the cursed part of that."

"Curst?"

"Yeah. Lesbians are like…homosexual. As in, they like the same gender. Girls like girls. Boys like boys. If's she's full lesbian…uh…you might consider not turning her at all. Just let her go. An eternity of celibacy has to be better than a forever reminder of what might be available and ready, but you can't have it."

"Excuse me?"

"But if she's bi-sexual! Oh…*baby!* If she swings either way, then your luck knows no bounds! You are going to get involved in girl-on-girl action and three-ways like…whenever you want. Forever."

"Three-ways?"

"Two women with one guy – that would be you. Picture the three of you. All naked. Limbs entwined. On a king-sized bed. Or…maybe in a large shower. Using tongues. Body parts. Uh…maybe even manual stimulation equipment. Imagine the positions! Any. All. Wow. You lucky bastard. I don't even have a woman around, and you'll get two of them."

"You're talking...*copulation?*"

Akron was laughing. Wystan was reeling. Images of what Nigel was describing, were warring with building rage at Nigel even thinking about Wystan's mate in that capacity. Especially naked. The sensation he'd felt moments earlier got hotter. Incensed. Furious. If this was emotion, it was bad. The view of his crypt got washed with blood-red hues on every eye blink, while flickers of fire ate through him. He was breathing deeply and harshly, his lips open, allowing room for the fangs that were almost at full length. Akron spoke next.

"You sound as if you know a bit about this subject, Nigel. I had no idea the Seventies were so enlightened."

"I have a vivid imagination, sir. Good thing, since I don't have women around me, like ever."

"Aren't we forgetting Lizbeth?"

"Oh. Come on. She doesn't count. She isn't remotely womanly. She's more like...a walking computer with boobs."

"We're almost out of time again. *De* Crecy? We'll call you back."

Akron was laughing again. Wystan tightened his fist so that the phone fizzled, sending heat through his hand and lower arm. He pitched it against a wall, where it exploded in a shower that contained plastic bits and blackened circuitry. His eyes narrowed as he watched the last sparks die on the stone floor.

Another phone vibrated and then it started singing in a high voice. Wystan grabbed it and pressed the "call" button just to shut it off.

"*De* Crecy? Good. You're still with us. I hope you'll forgive Nigel."

Akron was still chuckling. It wasn't remotely funny. Wystan didn't reply.

"I've got good news for you, however. You there?"

"Yes." The word was short. Clipped.

"You angry?"

"Yes."

"Apologies. I should've handled it. I hope this helps. Every covert action has some falsehoods about it. This sting was no exception. You follow?"

"No."

"The woman you met tonight was acting. Some of what happened might be real, some false."

"This is not helping," Wystan informed him.

"I was researching while Nigel was shooting off his mouth. Miss Rachel Berne doesn't have much on record, but she did file charges against a boyfriend last year. That does mean, even if she claims lesbianism, at one point she liked men."

"I am getting more angered," Wystan informed him.

"Very well. I'll talk faster. The woman named Eleanor Munson? Well, that woman has a husband. That should be even more help. Yes?"

A cooling sensation started in the pit of his belly and spread outward. It probably showed in his one-word answer.

"Yes."

"Good. Luckily, your mate is still on the premises. I took the liberty of having a message delivered to her. She's invited to an incredibly late visit at your castle. You might wish to dress in something a bit more appropriate. I hope this information helps a bit. *De* Crecy? You there?"

The phone went silent from where he'd dropped it. He didn't waste time ending the call. He could fetch it later. He had to reach his castle. And prepare.

CHAPTER SIX

"Thanks for giving me full credit for the bust. I owe you."

"He won't be harming little boys from where he's going. That's what matters."

Rachel didn't look up from her pseudo-tankard of spiced mead as she spoke. The tankard was crafted of heavy plastic. Fake. Just like almost everything around her. They were sitting on benches that looked like they'd come from the nearest kiddie park, under an enormous tent that looked machine-crafted, and watching some guys at one end sing raucous lyrics set to tunes they coaxed from some odd-looking instruments. It probably would've been better if they'd foregone the amplifier and microphone system, but they'd have been drowned out by the noise, otherwise. The place was doing a brisk business. Still. Everywhere she looked, people were having a good time. Or faking it.

Not Rachel.

She felt flat. Dull. Empty. Everything seemed murky and dark. Maybe it was due to the smoke coming off barrels of oil they'd placed all about the area. Or, it could be the torches sputtering away in their brackets from spikes that had been stuck into the ground. Good thing they had both ends of the tent open. They needed the fresh air.

"You know…instead of looking at that drink, you could enjoy it. Or we might as well get back to the hotel," Eleanor told her.

"You don't have to stay."

"And I thought you hated that outfit. Couldn't wait…to get it off."

"Yeah. I did." Rachel started pulling hairpins from her hair with one hand. The other lifted her mead. Took a sip. It was good stuff. Smooth. Sweet. Tasty.

"I don't suppose you got his name?" Eleanor asked.

Rachel's throat stopped on the swallow. Her heart followed suit. She had to force the mead down to reply.

"Who?" she asked in a nonchalant tone.

"The guy at your feet. The one in leather shoulder pads, gray-shaded tights, and kick-ass sword. The guy with the fantastic abs. And chest. And arms. And legs. Oh, screw it. I'm going to say…just about all of him was fantastic. That one."

"Oh. I got his name."

"Sweet!"

"Look. Munson. Can we talk of something else?"

"Right. Like that's going to work on me. I do interrogations in my sleep. So. Why the long face, honey? You got his name. Did you get his number?"

Rachel put the tankard back down on the tabletop, avoiding a sticky spot some earlier drinker had left. They didn't use tablecloths in here. It would be a waste. They'd be closing this place down in a couple of hours. Probably to clean up.

She worked the last of her hairpins free and pulled the hat off. She immediately straightened as if a great weight had come off her. She didn't take down or unfasten her braids. They didn't make her top-heavy. She wrapped the gauze about the cone-thing before putting it in her lap. She was stalling. It didn't work. Munson was right. She was a great interrogator. The Brits probably should've requested her help with that part of the operation as well.

"You know…we've got all night," Munson said.

"He said he didn't have a number."

"That's ridiculous."

"I know."

"Oh. Shit. I'm sorry. Sounds like he gave you the brush-off. The bastard. Give me his name. I'll put out a warrant on him."

"It's okay. Really. I mean, what am I supposed to do with him anyway?"

Her companion sputtered, and then laughed pretty heartily. "Oh. This is rich. Here I thought you were an edgy type. What do you do with him? You handcuff him to a bedpost and take him for a test drive. And he looked perfectly capable of handling anything on your roads. Hell. If I wasn't married, I'd help."

"I mean after the sex. Then what? Logistically speaking, it's better this way. Really."

"Bullshit. With a capital 'B'."

Eleanor opened the little purse she'd secured under her belt, took out a little silver canteen, unscrewed the top, and poured something into her tankard. Rachel watched without comment. *Well.* That explained why mead was kicking Eleanor's ass.

"Munson. I'm a New Yorker. He's a Brit."

"So?"

"I have a life."

"Right. Allow me to point out that you have a teeny apartment, no close relatives, and the same specter of breast cancer that took your mother hovering over you. Some life."

"Are you trying to depress me?"

"Nope. Just pointing out the obvious. Your life is a dead-end hamster wheel going nowhere. Why else would you be spending your vacation chasing a pedophile?"

"Because the bastard was not slipping away again."

"Oh, Rachel. Forgive me. I shouldn't talk and drink. My mouth is in gear and my brain isn't driving. Feel free to smack me anytime."

Eleanor Munson took a deep draught from her tankard. She obviously wasn't planning to drive anywhere. That was okay. Rachel was completely sober. She'd have them at their hotel in London probably before sun-up.

"His name was Wystan. Wystan, Something-or-other, Crecy."

Eleanor spewed her swallow, and then started choking. It wasn't faked. Rachel was rising to assist before she got waved off.

"Holy…crime shit. Wystan Ryn *de* Crecy? Do you know…who that is?"

"Sounded familiar. Should I know it?"

"Pull out your entry pass. Look at it."

That piece of paper was wadded into a pocket next to the cuffs she'd misplaced earlier. Rachel took it out, smoothed it, and then lifted it, squinting at the ornate printing. The light was terrible for people watching. It was ridiculously awful for reading.

"Okay. It says 'Ticket holder is entitled to the entire weekend at the Winter Renaissance Faire at Castle…Crecy'. We're at Castle Crecy? No. He can't. Are you going to tell me that guy *owns* this place?"

Munson nodded. "You really should read more of the stuff I do."

"I don't like tabloid fodder."

"If that guy was Sir Wystan *de* Crecy? Wow. I mean double wow. He's like, one of the country's most eligible bachelors. Should I mention he's a millionaire, too? Maybe I should make that billionaire. Nobody knows for certain. He's exceptionally secretive. Reclusive. And…oh man. I had no idea. The guy is such an introvert, he's like a ghost. He's never photographed. Never interviewed. Hell…if I'd known that was what he looked like? If anyone knew what he looked like? We wouldn't be able to get through the crowd of women surrounding the place."

"Must you?"

"Oh. I'm sorry. I'm supposed to be maligning the guy. He's a jerk. With incredibly poor eyesight.

I mean…how could he overlook you? In that dress? Wait. This looks promising."

"What?"

"There is a butler-looking fellow in the doorway. He's focusing on us. Yes. I was right. Here he comes."

"You are so full of it."

Despite her words, Rachel looked. There really was an elderly fellow weaving through the tables. He was wearing a perfectly ironed dark suit and carrying a polished silver tray. He reached the end of their table and executed a little dip of his head toward her. That was cute.

"Good morning. You are the Lady Rachel Berne?"

"Uh…"

"Say yes!" Munson hissed it.

Rachel chuckled a bit. *Why not?*

"Yes," she answered. And then wondered if she should get up and curtsey or something.

"I have a note for you. My lady."

He lowered his tray so she could lift the envelope resting there. Wow. It was made from very heavy paper. Embossed. Sealed. And it had been resting on a bed of what looked like rose petals.

Rachel broke the seal, lifted the flap, pulled out a page, and unfolded it to reveal the most incredible script. Her eyes widened. She'd seen this kind of calligraphy in books, but she'd never really envisioned receiving anything written in it. Her hand trembled.

"Well? What does it say?" Eleanor asked.

"I'm being invited to the castle."

"Oh, sweet! Holy sh—! I mean…crap. This is the most amazing thing I've ever seen. Is this classy, or what?"

"The invitation is extended to my friend, as well. You."

"Well. Hell. What are we waiting for?" Eleanor stood up, wobbled, and immediately slapped both hands on the tabletop to keep from falling.

"You want to wait a bit?" Rachel asked.

"Oh, hell no. Give me your arm. I'll be fine. Better than fine. I only wish I'd charged my phone so I could film some of this. Berne…we're going to a *castle*!"

The butler guy didn't change expression at Munson's words. That was impressive. Rachel tucked the bundle of her headdress and veil under one arm and walked around the table to offer the other one to Munson.

They made a weird procession through the crowd and out onto the grounds. The castle seemed to be a long way away. Or something. It also got quieter, a lot colder, and a lot dimmer, the further they walked from the faire. Not that it was overly dark. There was a full moon in the sky, sending silver tones onto everything. It glinted off a layer of frosted mist attempting to obscure the cobblestone path they walked, sent illumination onto the three-story-high walls they walked beside. It framed the high, arched gateway they walked through.

The first view of the castle was electrifying. Moonlight enveloped it in silvery hues. Everything that had felt dull and lifeless in Rachel went instantly alert and aware. Or something. Castle Crecy was jaw dropping. Breathtaking. Stunning.

An enormous edifice of impenetrable stone. Lights gleamed through some of the slits in the second story, as well as what looked like a round tower at one end. Rachel felt a chill cross her exposed chest and neck. It crept along her spine, worrying her. It was akin to the sixth sense that kept her out of all kinds of trouble.

Stifling it wasn't easy.

A wooden double-door marked the entrance, set in a recessed arch. It was at the top of a wide staircase of ten stone steps. Rachel tightened her grip on the *hennin* bundle in order to lift her skirts. Then she started climbing, pausing for Eleanor at each step. The butler waited for them at the doorway, holding one side open. They were probably on the second floor. Maybe. Rachel wasn't a castle junkie, nor was she a history buff, but this looked pretty damned impressive. And authentic.

The landing was even more impressive. Rachel stopped just inside the door, trying to take it all in, while Eleanor swayed at her side. She'd never seen such space, except maybe in a cathedral. The foyer area looked really high. There were window slits all about the upper roof edge, sending moonlight onto what looked like a series of banners hanging in rows, infusing the area with color.

"I am so hanging with you, Berne. From now on. You…and me. You need a companion on your next vacation…you call me. You hear?"

"What?" Rachel looked down at Munson.

"I mean…look at this. Just look." Eleanor's voice carried the awe Rachel was feeling. "We're in a real castle! And holy shit. Have you ever seen anything like this? I mean…outside of history books?"

"If you ladies would follow me, please?"

The butler had traversed the area, and stood patiently waiting for them at the opposite end. The door he held open led to a lighted space. It sent an off-kilter, rectangular chunk of light onto the polished stone floor. That served to make the shadows of the foyer suddenly look dark and foreboding.

Ominous.

Almost…threatening.

Another chill ran up Rachel's spine. She stood straighter and ignored it. And then she offered her arm to her companion again.

CHAPTER SEVEN

Where was she?

Wystan contemplated a sword display arranged on the wall just to the right of a fireplace. Not for any particular reason. It was just another attempt to ignore an anxious, on-edge feeling that had started up in the crypt and increased while he'd dressed. It was a new sensation. Odd. He'd spent countless hours in a state of limbo, watching the days, and then the years, and then the centuries, pass. Time lost meaning ever since he'd taken a lance in his side and accepted vampirism over death. Time hadn't any power. Or substance. Or weight. Yet, at the moment, he swore he could feel every second that passed as if there was a timing gear in him somewhere, and it just kept getting cranked tighter and tighter…

She wouldn't turn down his invitation, would she? Maybe he should have taken it to her personally. Maybe he should—

Stop, Wystan. It's been three minutes.

Maybe the mantel clock was broken. Why else would three minutes feel so long?

Wystan pulled in a deep breath. He didn't need it. He was just testing. And it worked. He really could breathe. It was incredible. Still. The velvet doublet he'd fastened didn't have much room for the move, however. It restricted his chest. It had a row of black satin ribbons securing both sides. Wystan grinned as one bow after the other pulled tight. Because he could *feel* that, too!

He probably should have worn material that had some give to it. He had plenty of options in his closets. But he'd selected this seventeenth century outfit, because it matched what she'd been wearing.

Sort of.

Actually, she'd been wearing attire that was a mish-mash from several eras. It hadn't mattered. She'd looked perfect. Better than perfect. That dark fabric hadn't disguised a feminine form, while the white linen ruffle of her bodice graced a womanliness he'd rarely beheld. She'd been the perfect height, her waist a hand-spanning size, while her bosom...

Oh...my!

Wystan stared down in absolute amazement as his loins stirred, straining against the tight knee breeches he'd donned. By all the saints! That was true, too! Such a thing was astounding. Unbelievable. And uncontrollable at present. Maybe if he'd had more time to adjust, he could keep this amount of lust tamped, or at least hidden. Somehow. He'd been right about wool, too. It itched. Maybe he should have donned under-drawers.

He glanced at the clock again.

Another minute gone.

Oh. This was bad form. Wystan put a hand to his crotch area and pulled, trying to rearrange and gain some room. Then he pulled the waist of his coat down a bit, stretching seams. Well. Apparently, they hadn't tailored masculine attire in the 1600s to disguise a man if he enlarged for any reason. *Bother.* The last thing he wanted was to look like a stag in rutting season when she arrived. He'd be better off examining the swords. And if that didn't work, he supposed he could pull down a shield from another display and hide behind it.

Look over the swords.

Yes. That was it. Examine the swords. And then he was facing another oddity. Checking weaponry used to be an engrossing, time-consuming activity. There was always something that needed to be seen to. Some flaw to be corrected. Oxidation to remove. Corrosion to eradicate. But at the moment, looking over swords was worse than troublesome. It was downright suggestive. They brought to mind what more than one literary source claimed a sword represented to society in general. They were representative of a phallus.

An erect phallus.

Merde! This wasn't working.

Wystan narrowed his eyes and leaned closer to the sword display. These blades came mostly from the fourteenth century. They had thick, non-ornamented, grip-friendly hilts. They'd seen a lot of use…probably in some nameless battle. Back when they still used swords. He used to join in if the day was dark enough, and he was bored.

Oh. Look there.

Although expertly polished and maintained, more than one blade showed signs of deterioration. They might have been fashioned of inferior iron. He should probably move those blades to the armory, and work on them.

The door opened behind him.

Wystan spun.

"Sir Wystan? May I present the Lady Rachel Berne? And her companion."

Wystan probably shouldn't have been touching anything. One blade fell. He caught it. He snagged the two that followed, but that just seemed a signal for the entire display to collapse like water breaking through a dam. One after another they fell, in a litany of clanking. Before he knew it, there was a mound of weaponry at his feet and a lot of noise announcing that fact. And just when had he gotten so clumsy?

Somebody giggled. It sure as hell wasn't him. He was discovering that embarrassment was a pretty good panacea for lust. Actually, it was an excellent one. Wystan considered the stack of blades at his feet for several seconds, before he stepped right over them.

"Um...hello?"

Wystan glanced up as his mate spoke. The next moment he was right in front of her, and if he hadn't been holding three swords, he'd have probably gone to his knee again. As it was, he just stood there, swallowing hard, as if studying the braids coiled atop her head. He ignored the sword blades that dangled from his hands as well as the woman clinging to his mate's arm.

Damn everything. He couldn't control movement better than this?

"You have a very…um…yeah. Your castle. It's…wow."

Wystan moved his gaze down to hers. How had he failed to notice she had such unique eyes? They were so light blue, they looked like liquid silver, and surrounded by thick lashes of dark brown that matched her hair. He'd never seen such incredible eyes. Clear. Fathomless. Containing all the mysteries of the universe. He could lose himself in her gaze. And almost did. She blinked, and then blushed, putting a pink tinge to her cheeks that matched her lips. He'd been mistaken. She was worse than beautiful. She was amazingly beautiful.

"Sir…Crecy?"

The woman at his mate's side spoke, snagging his attention. She was gripping his mate's arm like she belonged there. Wystan's eyes narrowed. He barely caught and stopped the tingle of his canines. He focused on stanching that, rather than ripping the Munson woman's hands away from his mate. He didn't know anything of this lesbian thing. He knew less of women. Akron had said this Eleanor person was wed. Right now, said husband was close to becoming a widower.

"Pleased…to meet you."

The woman released his mate and curtsied awkwardly. She didn't look very steady on her feet. Her words had been slurred, as well. Is that why she held onto his mate's arm? She was inebriated? The woman lifted her hand toward him. Wystan automatically took it and brought it toward his lips. He didn't kiss it. His kisses belonged to just one woman. He dropped her hand. The woman giggled again. And then she hiccupped, although she hid it behind her hand.

"Do you have some...place where I could...sit down?"

Wystan glanced at his mate. Her eyebrows rose up and down several times as if conveying him a message. He didn't understand. She smiled next.

"Um...Eleanor did a bit too much celebrating. She needs to rest. And maybe sip on a glass of water, as well?"

"Ah. A place to rest. Most assuredly, ladies."

Both women jumped at his words. Wystan had a tremendous voice. Deep. Soul-stirring. Most vampires did. And worse. His couldn't quite conceal what had to be joy as he realized the obvious. His mate wasn't exhibiting lesbian behavior. The women were simply friends, and she was giving an assist.

He'd selected this room for its beauty. It was small in comparison to the rest of the castle. It had an aura of coziness and tranquility. It also led directly to a series of chambers he called the Georgian Wing. He'd had it designed during the American Revolutionary War period, when he'd been portraying an invalided *de* Crecy. That particular suite of rooms contained not one, but two bedchambers, both with giant canopied beds – a fact he'd tried to pretend didn't matter.

The one thing he hadn't taken into consideration was the salon's acoustical properties. Wystan cleared his throat and attempted a higher, softer range of voice. It sounded ridiculous even to his ears.

"Would a...sofa be acceptable?"

Wystan turned sideways to reveal the room. He'd ordered a fire set. It had finally caught, putting welcome warmth into the space. Directly in its glow was a seating arrangement of cream-shaded, brocade-covered pieces: a sofa, two loveseats, three chairs. There were several French-styled occasional tables as well. Barring the mound of weaponry he'd created, the space still looked inviting and personable.

"Perfect." His mate replied. "And...perhaps she could get a comforter?"

Comforter. What the devil was that?

"A blanket?"

She answered his unspoken question.

"Oh. Yes. I'll see one fetched."

He needed to concentrate on his movements! He was at the door and signaling a servant before the ladies even took a step toward the furniture. He was in luck that his mate wasn't looking.

Calm down, Wystan.

He needed to use slow, studied movements. Employ soft tones when speaking. Keep any lustful thoughts at bay. Act like a normal man. Mortal. His servant handed him a folded woven blanket. Wystan bent his arms to receive it. Then he turned, took a step, and was back with the ladies with the very next one. The women hadn't even been seated yet. He'd never failed quite so ignobly before.

Actually...he'd never failed at all.

Wystan's back straightened as he realized it. This mating thing was beyond control and comprehension. He watched as the Munson woman collapsed onto the sofa. Then she reclined, and before his mate even turned to take the blanket from him, the woman was snoring.

Snoring?

Wystan hadn't been around women. This was the first time he'd heard one snore. His mate spent a bit of time arranging the blanket about her companion, giving him way too much view of her slender waist. Nice-sized backside. He could just imagine what her breasts might look like as that bodice took the brunt of the weight and volume with her movements.

Damn these wool breeches.

His mate turned back to him. She'd pulled her bottom lip between her teeth. Deep rose shaded the tops of her cheeks. Wystan rocked in place, making the sword blades clank against each other. He was still holding three swords? And he hadn't even noticed?

"Um. Thank you. For the blanket…and the help tonight…and…"

She tipped her gaze to his. A roar of noise whooshed through his ears, obliterating her words. He frowned to make them more audible, and her voice stopped. She looked away from him, giving him a perfect view of her lashes dusting her cheeks. While below that, her bountiful bosom moved with each breath. Framed by ruffles. Lifted. Displayed.

Tempting…

She flashed a glance to him and then away again. Toward the fire. A surge of something unbelievably vast hit him, knocking him a fell step backward. He'd never dealt with such a thing. Everywhere he looked and everything he tried, and every place he sent his mind to seemed to contain the same things:

Pure, unadulterated need. Massive want. Uncontrollable craving.

Oh, no.

His canines were more than tingling. They were elongating, pressing against his inner lip. Nothing he tried stopped it. He wanted her *now*. Right now. He very nearly reached out and seized her. He wanted her locked in his arms, her curves pressed to him. Her mouth against his. So he could taste. Savor. Devour. He needed his arms and legs entwined with hers. Sans clothing. Naked flesh touching...

He was beset with images. His body slamming into hers. Her loins accepting every thrust. Experiencing her cavern. Claiming. Owning.

His breathing grew strident and harsh, while the wool knee breeches took the brunt of this arousal. Someone should have warned him about the realities of finding one's mate. The frightening scope of physical reaction it engendered. Wystan locked every muscle at his command for control. He was shaking. The only reason the swords didn't rattle against each other was because he held the hilts so tightly they twisted in his hands. And then one blade came loose from its housing and fell, spearing the floor between them.

"Wystan?"

Her breath touched him like a physical force. He steeled himself to endure the next. And then the next. And then he had to answer.

"Yes?"

Oh. Hell. He wasn't disguising anything. Saying that one word hurt his throat. It was bestial deep. Sinful black. Harsh. Guttural.

"Thank you…for inviting me. Um…into your home."

He groaned. The sound resounded through the room. It barely covered over the sound of the last two swords as they fell.

CHAPTER EIGHT

The room reverberated with the deep bass tones of his voice. They lingered for long moments before dying out. Rachel trembled in place and tried to absorb it. And him. She'd never come up against such a male specimen. Or such a situation. She doubted any woman had.

Wow.

Make that double wow. And then add a smack for good measure.

Sir Wystan *de* Crecy was a lot of man. He'd changed clothes. It didn't help. He might as well be standing half-naked before her like before, his chest and belly heaving visually with every breath. He was doing unbelievable things to her hormones. Every cell seemed to be dancing in anticipation. Or something. And this linen bodice material was way too stimulating against her nipples! Rachel had handled all kinds of men. All kinds of sexual situations. This was the first time she'd felt anything approaching the electrical current that seemed to emanate from Wystan and strike right at the deepest part of her.

"You're the…shy type, aren't you?"   She ventured the question.

"No."

His answer came in an unbelievably deep tone. She'd never heard such a voice from a real throat. It sounded like he was sending it through a synthesizer or something. Gooseflesh raced along her skin. He kept his gaze fastened on something beyond the top of her head. And then she watched his Adams Apple move as he gulped.

"It's okay if you are. Really. It…explains a lot."

She stepped closer, daring contact, then licked her lower lip. She felt like a teen again. On the precipice of sexual discovery. *Weird.* She had experience. She'd done a few one-night stands. They'd left her physically satisfied and emotionally blank. She'd sworn off them. But something odd was happening here. Something beyond her grasp of understanding.

She was actually considering sex with some guy she'd just met?

Wait.

She wasn't just considering it. She was damn near instigating it. Oh, but she felt wicked. Free. Uninhibited. And out-of-this-world excited. She felt young again and twice as giggly. Oh. This was going to be amazing fun. Stupendous fun. More fun than she'd ever had before.

She had to force the giddiness down in order to form words.

"Well, Wystan. I…have some experience. I've met…all kinds of personalities. I'd heard you were an introvert. And a recluse. I'm thinking shyness goes pretty much hand-in-hand with those."

He grunted something that might be an answer. The hairs on the back of her neck rose in response. The man exuded sex appeal with every passing moment. It was juxtaposed with desire that dripped from every syllable she managed to coax from his lips. And then he sent everything ratcheting higher with how his chest rose and fell with each harsh breath.

"Look at me, Wystan."

He shook his head. Rachel looked up to study him. She was tall. Five-nine was almost catwalk-model height. But he was a hell of a lot taller. Firelight put all kinds of definition to him, too, casting a ridge along his nose, a fringe of spiky shadow from his lashes onto his cheeks. Her entire frame pulsed toward him. Now, *that* she'd never felt before. She got bolder, moving her index finger toward the spot where his vest-thing met the mass of material wound about his throat.

"Why not?"

"I...can't explain."

He answered with a tone that sent throbs of something tangible through the room. They encompassed Munson's snoring. The firelight. The slightest scent of rose petals lingering in the air. Rachel touched his neck cloth, and then wove her fingers into the folds, using it as a handhold to get just the slightest bit closer. Close enough to get singed.

"Why not?" she asked again.

He glanced down at her before studying something over her head. The earth shifted. The world spun. Rachel swayed in place, held there by her fingers entwined with his cravat. The look she'd received was akin to a physical force. His pupils hadn't looked remotely black. They'd contained flame – blue-white at the center – and twice as hot. He'd shot absolute fire all the way through her. It scorched. Electrified. And she couldn't gain any air!

Rachel's lips parted to gain breath. Her heart pained. Her head rocked backwards. She felt like a liquid, ephemeral being.

Wild. Unfettered. Uncontrolled.

And nothing like herself

"There's a beast within me," he finally replied.

Rachel laughed. It wasn't a gay sound. It resembled a harpy who'd found her mark. A siren who'd honed in on her doomed sailor. A sorceress who'd spied her victim. And he was spouting nonsense. But it was a full moon. She was on ancient soil. In an awe-inspiring castle. Amidst all sorts of arcane symbolism. In virtual isolation…with a stranger.

Anything seemed possible.

"You mean…like a werewolf?" she asked, not even questioning the insanity behind such a query.

"No."

His hands closed about her waist in order to pull her toward him. The exposed flesh above her bodice came into contact with the smooth surface of his velvet jacket. Her fingers gripped tighter to his neck cloth, her legs slammed against his. She could swear she could feel him. Hard. Muscular. Unrelenting. Even through all the layers of fabric swathed about her. And then he lowered his head. Rachel's eyes went wide on what looked like long, amazingly white fangs. Real…

…fangs.

Holy shit.

"Like a vampire," he said. And then he lowered his head and stabbed them into her neck.

Rachel cried out in shock. It changed almost immediately to a long moan as absolute ecstasy overtook every other sensation. Pleasure filled her, coming in waves that matched how he sucked at her neck, pulling at her life's fluid, sending rapture shooting through her veins. She'd never felt anything like it. The feeling encased, and enshrouded, and then demanded. Every bit of experience she ever had got shredded and then dispersed, like so many ashes tossed to the wind. Rachel was reeling. Spinning into a vortex of black.

And then it changed. Making a kaleidoscope of color.

She was falling…

Cool sheets met her back. Deep pockets of comfort supported her. *Ah.* She was atop an enormous mattress. In a bed chamber. A quick scan showed all sizes and heights of bureaus and armoires and dressers, their surfaces covered with hundreds of lit candles situated in dozens of candelabra.

Oh my.

Rachel had never seen anything like it. Candlelight reached through the gauzy material of the canopy, lighting the enclosure with a myriad of golden flickers. It was beautiful. Amazing. Private. Giving an instant impression of an oasis in a sea of castle; a haven in the midst of chaos; a private niche of space; a pagan altar on which to worship. Adore.

Consummate…

Her vision filled with Wystan. But it wasn't the man she'd been conversing with. Oh. No. This was an intensely sexier version. He was on his knees, facing her. As she watched, he yanked the vest-thing over his head, ripping something, while ruffling the perfect fall of his hair. He chucked the garment somewhere behind him. He didn't check. She didn't either. He didn't move his gaze from hers. And she was captivated. Mesmerized. Fascinated.

He was wearing medieval fashion. His sleeves weren't sewn to his shirt. They appeared to be tied on at the shoulders and under the arms with little bows of like-shaded fabric. He ignored the ties, and jerked at each sleeve, sending more ripping noise into the enclosure as he pulled them off his arms and sent them over his shoulder to the same place his vest had landed.

Somewhere music started up, filling the space with a swell of sound. A drum thumped to a beat that dragged her heart into rhythm with it. An oboe sent trills along her skin in accompaniment. A flute stirred her thoughts, meshing reality with fantasy. And at the center of the orchestration was Wystan. The remaining piece of fabric he wore for a shirt was wrenched apart and discarded, making muscles ripple throughout his chest. Arms. Abdomen. This guy definitely had abs to die for. Rachel was running her fingers along them the moment he put them on display.

He caught a hand, and brought it to his lips, to place a kiss atop her knuckles. He turned her hand over and traced his tongue in a whorl shape along her palm. A blizzard of shivers raced up her arm.

Hit her breasts. Sent her nipples into erect nubs that rubbed against the linen bodice. And then he punctuated everything. Before she could grasp it, he stabbed his fangs into the vein at her wrist.

And then he was sucking and licking, and sending all sorts of sensation with every flick of his tongue.

Rachel writhed and moaned along the bed. Her eyes still locked to his. But his no longer contained anything red. Or fiery. They were solid black. Deep. Dark. Sensual. Relentless. He pulled from the incision he'd made, licking it into nothing more than two, slightly pink spots, and then he lowered his chin and regarded her. Oh! That look stole her ability to breathe. Think. Do anything other than gape.

"My mate. My…one. True. Mate."

His words ended with another bit of adulation, this time along her arm. His kiss moved over her wristwatch and then up her arm, under the billowy drape of her sleeve. Rachel flung her head back in a meager search for air. Any air. As much as she could gain. As quickly as she could pull it in. And then he was there. All of him. Solid male. Hard. Muscled. Spectacular. She roamed her hands about his torso, amazed and emboldened by how his skin flinched and jerked with her touch.

His mouth had hers.

Or was it the other way around?

Rachel was panting. Sucking. Dueling with his tongue. She felt a pinprick of pain. Had he really cut her? And then nothing mattered as more throes of pleasure hit. And they just got more intense as the kiss deepened. Nothing had ever felt so glorious. Ever.

"How do you unfasten your corset?"

He mouthed it along her lips. Rachel licked at him, tasting something metallic. Salty.

Was that blood?

"How?"

His voice got more demanding. The kiss that followed it had the same intent. Demanding. Unrelenting. Insistent.

"Ties. At the back."

He flipped her over without a hint of effort. But he wasn't pulling the little bows apart. She felt the instant pressure just before the release as he simply ripped the entire cross-lacing apart. The corset thing went sailing over the side of the bed. She didn't even miss it. He was spooned about her, his hands cupping and supporting her linen-covered breasts, while every inhalation he made sent his pecs into her back. And then he was rolling, pulling her atop him. Back-to-front. Not once did he release the torment of her nipples. His thumbs and fingers kept massaging. Kneading. And driving her absolutely mad with anticipation. Rachel's cries tore her throat. Her thrashing gained her little. He easily held her in place atop him, while stabbing at her backside with his cock.

And that was changing.

Rachel grabbed his hands, and pulled them away. And he let her. She spun, and then she was straddling him, panting with effort as she looked down at him. *Wow.* There was no better word. Wystan was gorgeous. More sculpted statue than man. Rachel's throat pinched off, her eyes stung with what couldn't possibly be tears, and her heart pulsed with a heave that almost hurt. All of that was just ridiculous. This was an aberration…not only of time and space and her personal code of behavior.

It was also beyond the realm of possibility.

No man was this sexy. No man was this handsome.

She rose and fell with each of his breaths. Her legs were still encased in yards of material. The hips she straddled were also clothed. And it felt completely erotic. Sensual. Exciting.

"Ah. Rachel. My love. My…mate."

The words were huffed between lips that looked swollen and stained with blood. That wasn't likely or possible. She didn't believe in fate. She didn't believe in vampires. And she sure as hell didn't believe in love at first sight. He couldn't possibly mean what she thought he'd said. And if he was that naïve, he was in for a nasty surprise. This was a one-night stand.

Not a commitment.

Rachel leaned down to hover atop him, her mouth just out of reach. Open. Grasping. Breathing with him. She flicked a tongue out and connected with his lip. He jerked, lifting them completely off the mattress, while the moan that ensued scored through both of them.

And that was like lighting the fuse. She needed to experience all of him. Deep. And right now.

Now.

He got the message without words. Rachel rolled to her side in order to tug on the ties of her waistband with fingers that trembled. She shoved the skirts down, shimmying out of the first layer, using hands that shook. The second layer followed. Then the last. And then she was unclasping the buckle on her thigh holster. She shoved it up under one of the pillows. The boots had to go next and those buttons up her ankles gave her all kinds of trouble.

Damn medieval fashion!

She probably should have just taken her knife blade to the stupid things. But finally, it was done. Rachel tossed the boots toward the side of the mattress, watched them disappear, and heard a distinct thud as they landed somewhere on the floor. That left her nothing other than the insubstantial item Munson had called a chemise.

And…wow.

Wystan hadn't been idle. His knee breeches were gone and he was stretched out on his back, displaying a cock that was erect, and filled, and pretty damned enormous. Rachel's jaw dropped, and her eyes widened. Holy shit. Wystan was unbelievably well-built. Thick. Hard. And ready.

Rachel hiked her chemise up, flung a leg over him, aimed, and then…

Oh my!

Nothing had prepared her for the sensation of fullness. Wystan lurched upward as she encased him, the move shoving further into her, while the groan that resonated from him filled the enclosure with sound. And he was shaking. The bedstead rattled with it.

"Oh, love! Oh…Rachel. Oh…love!"

He matched the words to his motions. His hands grabbed her ass and lifted her. Held her posed above him for countless moments where everything seemed to halt, and then he hauled her back down. Impaling her. Filling. Creating.

The throbs of sound got louder. Harsher. Deeper. Wystan must be hearing it, too, for his rhythm matched every beat. Every thump. Again. More. Harder. Every move slid ridges of definition into her. Again. And again. And then faster. Something sparked into being within her. It grew. Became an all-out wave of tension. And it came closer. Rachel grabbed onto his arms, tightened her thighs, flung her head back.

And careened into wonder.

Her cries had joy at their core. Laughter accompanied it as her body finished shuddering through throes of absolute delight. Mountains of ecstasy. Rivers of physical pleasure. And through it all, Wystan continued thrusting into her. Pulling her back down onto him. Lifting his hips to join them more fully. Raising her up again. Matching every one of her movements.

His dark eyes were waiting for her as the pleasure peaked and subsided, becoming once again a thrum of tension. Only this time, he shifted, rolling her beneath him, and pushing himself up, to put all that physique in perfect line-of sight.

And what a view!

Rachel caught her lower lip between her teeth, and ran both hands along every inch of him she could reach, before gripping her fingers into his upper arms. And still he continued pumping into her. Again. More. Harder. Rachel tightened her legs, and met each thrust.

Little grunts began to accompany his movements. They began as short pants of sound.

They steadily grew in length and volume. Her heart heard them first. Then her ears. And then her entire body. They accompanied his movements, pumping with a strength that shook the bed-frame, and jolted the mattress. Again. Harder. Deeper.

The mattress became a storm-tossed raft. An avalanche-tossed boulder. A tree in a hurricane's path.

Wystan's grunts grew keener. Sharper. Every muscle on display went tighter. Even more defined. And then he shoved a final time, arched backwards, lifting her, while the longest, deepest groan emitted from his throat. Snakes of veins stood out just beneath his skin.

His entire body pulsed volcanically, beginning within him, but ending in her.

Rachel was spellbound. Rapt. It was impossible to look away. Her heart was hammering like a wild thing within her chest as she watched.

And was caught watching.

She'd had sex before. She'd been the naïve one. She'd never had anything like this.

CHAPTER NINE

"Hey! Berne? You ever waking up? Or, do I have to come in there and fetch you?"

Rachel opened her eyes groggily. Blinked on a span of what looked like striped mattress ticking. Despite the dimness, she didn't have any trouble seeing perfectly. Better than perfectly. She could make out individual threads in the fabric weave.

Where the hell was she?

"You're missing some fantastic grub out here!"

Munson's voice filtered through the drapery framing the bed. The room was windowless and dark, except for the sliver of light where the door had been cracked open. It didn't hamper Rachel's vision at all. She could pick out all kinds of furniture pieces without squinting. There was a myriad of silver candelabra atop every surface. Everywhere. *Man.* That Wystan sure did know how to impress a girl. Dried wax had congealed in drip patterns all along the candle holder and trays. That was messy. Looked difficult to clean. Somebody was not going to be happy with that chore.

Rachel stretched. Sat. The comforter wrapped about her slid off her shoulders to her waist. She jerked it back up.

She was naked.

Oh. Shit.

Images of Wystan were immediate and fierce. All that man. All that muscle. All that bare flesh. Secured between her thighs. She almost expected to see him.

"I'm having a real English breakfast out here. I could use some help! I've got fried back bacon. English sausage. Grilled tomato. Fried bread. Poached eggs. Beans. And they delivered it on silver platters! This has got to match anything served at a five-star hotel! I am so not joking. You coming sometime today, or what?"

Rachel fought a gagging reflex. Everything Munson described came with an instant aroma. It smelled horrid. Stomach-turning. That was odd. She loved bacon. She rolled onto her belly, fishing beneath the lone pillow at the headboard. Her stungun was missing. Not a problem. So were the other eight or so pillows. She and Wystan had done some pretty fierce rocking in here. More than once. No doubt it had fallen somewhere. She'd just have to check…

An instant later she was standing at the side of the canopied bed. Rachel pushed the hair off her shoulder. *Oh yeah.* She remembered. Wystan had taken the braids out and finger-combed her hair. That had been erotic. A shiver whispered across her skin as she remembered. The man was amazingly gifted, packing some serious equipment, and majorly talented. It was almost a shame to relegate what had happened with him to the one-night stand file in her head. She really needed to get dressed, though. Find her taser. Join Munson.

Get back to reality…

She held the blanket about her with one hand while the other lifted the mattress. Nope. Nothing. She lifted the bed frame next, bending at the waist to look beneath it. Her holstered taser was just in sight. She reached in and snagged it. The structure creaked. It did worse when she released it. The posts thumped when they hit the floor. Now. To find her attire. *No*. Probably not. He'd shredded the chemise. The corset was a wash. The skirts were crumpled somewhere, but how could she wear them topless? And she could only see one boot. Maybe he had clothing in some of the drawers. Or the wardrobe closet-things. She was starting to get annoyed. This was so not funny.

Rachel took a step toward a dresser and arrived there on the next step. That had to been a good ten feet in distance. She blinked twice as she regarded the wax-coated candelabra sitting atop a five-drawer bureau. She moved that quickly?

Wait a minute. She'd just lifted a bed. What was it made of? Polystyrene? Was it a fake like everything down at the Renaissance Faire? It sure looked authentic. The feeling of unease that she should have listened to earlier was back, sending a solid chill up her spine. It was stronger than ever and twice as cold.

She put her holster on the dresser and started opening drawers. The top one contained socks and panties. Really sexy panties. In her size. Weird. She grabbed a pair of each. The second drawer held an array of bras, cups nestled together, packed in rows that resembled a color wheel. It looked like a lingerie display. Rachel sucked in on her bottom lip before lifting the nearest one. It was pink. It had beige lace all about it. She didn't see anything except the size. 36DD.

Hers.

Okay.

This was going beyond weird. It was getting downright bizarre. And slightly scary. Rachel donned the bra. Stepped into the panties. Shoved her feet into the socks, one after the other. The next drawer down had a selection of ankle-length pants. They were the kind that zipped up the back. They'd been sewn without a waistband, but had darts to shape them. And look. They were all in her size, too. She snagged out a dark pink pair.

The bottom drawer held mock-neck turtleneck sweaters. Good thing. She needed the warmth to counteract the shakes. She grabbed the first one and shoved it over her head, tugging her hair out with a move that made it sizzle with static electricity. Great. The top she'd picked was in another shade of pink. She probably looked ridiculous. She was beyond caring. Everything fit perfectly. No. Better than that. It fit like everything had been sewed to her exact dimensions.

The first armoire door she opened held shoes. Little ballet flats in patent leather black. They fit perfectly. *And...what do you know, Rachel?* There was also a little, quilted pink jacket with pink-shaded fur. And a matching hat.

She shoved the jacket on. Then the hat. Secreted the stun-gun in a lining pocket just beneath her bosom. She really needed some air. Some light. Some reassurance. Some grounding for reality.

Cripes!

Munson had every light lit in the outer room. Every single one. Rachel shaded her eyes when she stepped out. She'd been right. The smell of food was nauseating. Munson looked over and then started laughing. She almost choked on her bite. It wasn't funny.

"Wow, Berne! That is cute. You look like something out of a 60's ski-bunny movie. All you need is a pair of skis and a guy in tight black pants and a fair-isle sweater. Or a tuxedo. I wonder if we could get your new man to oblige?"

"Get up. We're leaving," Rachel said.

"Now?"

"Yeah. Right now."

"Well. I have a car coming for me. Should be here in…," Munson checked her phone. Shook it. Then put it back in her skirt pocket. "Damn thing's dead. Should have brought my charger cord, but who could have foreseen this?" She lifted an arm to encompass the room about her before going back to her plate.

"You have a car coming? Here or the faire? And when? When is the car coming?"

Munson tilted her head and regarded Rachel for some time. Rachel actually shifted, leaning her weight on her other hip and back. Damn! The woman was a good at interrogating.

"Yes, I have a car coming. They're sending it to the castle door. It will be here in about ten minutes. Fifteen, maybe."

"Too long."

"Surely we can compromise, Berne? Sit down. Drink some coffee. Have some bacon. It's perfectly fried."

Munson lifted a slice. Rachel swallowed on a vaguely ill feeling.

"Ten minutes. You said ten. Right?"

That might be enough. She'd be away from here before the sun set.

"About. I didn't have much battery power on my phone, and the reception stinks out here, but I got a message from New York. They woke me up. I'm booked on a red-eye tonight. I have to report back at the office Monday morning. I'm not on my vacation...like some people. I don't get another six days here."

"I'm going with you."

"You can't be serious."

"As a heart attack."

"Okay. Sir Wystan is a stick in the sack, despite every appearance to the contrary. That probably explains why he's a bachelor."

Rachel actually felt the blush. "I hope you don't expect an answer," she replied.

"Ah. He's puny then. Poor man."

"Eleanor."

"Maybe he's too quick to the finish?"

"Will you stop with the questions, and get moving?"

"I'm just trying to get the facts here. You're single. Beautiful. Available. You hooked up. No surprise there. Your new man has a voice that turns cream into butter, complete with a British accent. He's a kazillionaire. Classy. Highly secretive, but hell. I don't blame him. He'd be a paparazzo's dream. No tabloid would be complete without at least one picture. The guy is hot, Rachel. He's the hottest thing I've ever seen. He was born handsome, but he obviously works out, too. And now – according to you – we know he's well-hung, and great in the sack."

"I never said that."

"No need, honey. I read faces and body language. You going to answer the real question? The one about why you'd leave…without even saying goodbye?""

"What time is it?"

"Who cares? It's Saturday. We busted the bad guy. The world is clear of one more pervert. You should be celebrating. You're on vacation, remember?"

"When is it going to get dark?"

"Dark? It's winter, Berne. According to that weather report I got before my phone died, they're expecting a snowstorm. I'm sure the mead hall is doing bang-up business down at the faire."

"I mean sundown. When is sundown?"

Rachel's voice was rising. She ran her hands along her hips. She needed pockets on her pants. A male probably came up with these things. There wasn't much room for anything. They were great for showing off curves. Stupid design. Women should revolt.

"I don't know. An hour…maybe."

"An hour?" It was almost screeched.

"Shit, Berne. Keep your panties on. I have a hangover headache."

"But, you're breakfasting!"

"So, sue me. I slept in. Hell. If they hadn't called me, I'd probably still be sleeping. And after I found the loo – which is the second door on the right out in the hall, by the way – I came back in here. Lounged around for a bit. Checked for messages. Do you know they had part of a castle explode last night? Somewhere in Cornwall. Rock-something-or-other. Didn't get the details, but apparently a group of guys started a fire in an oil drum for warmth and ka-boom! A hunk of ruined castle gets more picturesque. Bodies burned beyond recognition.

"They're not saying terrorist, but something doesn't sound right. You know me, though. I would've read the entire newsflash, but my phone kept going in and out. That being the case, I did some exploring. Found where you'd gone to. And I have to say, you sure were sleeping soundly. Didn't hear a thing. So, I came back here. Pulled on the braided cord thingee by the fireplace. Some guy named Roderick showed up. I requested a full English breakfast. And there you have it. You really should try some. It's amazing."

"Uh…no thanks."

Munson had a bite of egg-topped toast halfway to her mouth. She stopped to look closely at Rachel. Too closely. "Something you want to tell me?"

She put the bite into her mouth and started chewing. Rachel's stomach gurgled in revolt. She barely kept from grimacing. She opened her mouth and then shut it. What was she supposed to say?

I had fantastic sex. Incredible. Mind-blowing. Then things got out of hand. I got bit by a vampire. Or…the shrink was right, and I'm over-stressed.

Maybe she was overreacting here. It had been years since her last one-night stand. If she remembered right, she'd always felt a little weird the next day. She might have eaten something that disagreed with her last night, hence the nausea. She could have been on an adrenaline kick that made movement and strength so odd. She could have imagined things...

Like fangs.

Maybe it *was* job stress, combined with jet-lag, and then excitement over the bust. It could be a sum total of the entire experience. She'd never been out of the states before. She'd never imagined she'd be in an actual castle. She'd never been surrounded by so much history. The entire place exuded a certain atmosphere and she'd only seen a fraction of it. It was medieval. Ancient. They'd driven through countryside that had something mystic and slightly other-worldly about it, too. Maybe she should give Wystan a chance. Find him and ask him point-blank about his claims of vampirism. The moment she saw him. That was the best time to catch anyone in a lie, before explanations could get invented.

"You wouldn't believe me if I told you," she finally said.

"Have a seat, Rachel. I'll pour you a cup of java. They make fantastic coffee here. What am I saying? Everything is top of the line. Top."

Coffee?

She'd gag.

"I'll wait for you at the front door."

Rachel took a step toward the door. She arrived there in a blink of time that blurred the view. She turned the knob. And Wystan was standing there.

CHAPTER TEN

Oh...*baby!*

He wasn't in tight black ski pants and a fair-isle patterned sweater or a tuxedo. He was wearing perfectly tailored dark slacks, a cream-shaded pullover knitted with really fine threads, and a sport coat. The pants didn't do a thing to hide muscled thighs, the sweater was falling from toned pecs, and the coat just defined his shoulder width. His hair was the perfect length. He had it pulled back into a queue at the moment, and that just put full illumination on what Munson had tried to describe. The guy wasn't just hot. He was absolutely gorgeous. And nothing about him looked remotely dangerous. Or sinister.

Or non-human.

Her body was doing all kinds of antics due to his presence. Her breath caught. Her throat tightened. Her clothing felt restrictive and confining. A quiver of something wondrously enticing started at the base of her spine and shot outward, reaching her scalp and her toes at roughly the same instant. She actually gravitated toward him without one bit of resistance.

He'd grinned the moment he saw her, showing off extremely white teeth. There wasn't anything sharp or odd about them. And then he sobered.

"You're leaving?"

"Uh…"

"My lady, please. I've so much to show you."

He put a hand out, palm upwards. Rachel glanced down at it and back to him. Her heart felt like it swooped downward before resuming its correct position. Amazing. She'd never responded to anything this way. She'd forgotten the effect of his eyes, too. Dark. Deep. Mysterious. And endlessly fascinating. She couldn't break contact, even if she wanted to.

And she didn't.

"Good afternoon, Your Grace! So wonderful to see you again."

Wystan looked over her shoulder, releasing the odd power of his gaze. He was frowning as he took in Munson's position. Rachel didn't have to check Munson's location. She was right behind her, pinching the back of Rachel's upper arm through her coat sleeve.

Wystan tipped his head in acknowledgement. "Please. Only a duke is referred to as such. I am a baron."

"A baron. Okay. What do you call a baron?"

"As I'm also a knight, you may call me Sir Wystan. Or, simply, Wystan."

"All right. Well. Thank you for your hospitality, Sir Wystan. Truly. We had a spectacular time. But we were just about to leave. Weren't we, Rachel? Rachel?"

"You would leave me?"

He turned his attention back to her to ask it. He still had his hand out, silently giving the entire decision to her. Her ears filled with a long note of swelling sound. And then he smiled again. *Oh.* The guy had a smile that would've sold any number of items if he'd marketed with it. Her entire body reacted, moistening like a parched bit of earth receiving its first raindrop of a storm, while tingling with the imminent danger of lightning that might be accompanying it.

She'd never felt such a thing. It was hopelessly addictive. She pulled her arm slightly, freeing it from Munson's touch. She'd been delusional. He was no more a vampire than she was. He couldn't be. They didn't exist. But the cop in her made her persist enough to make certain.

"Is the sun...down?" she asked him.

His smile deepened. His eyes grew more intense somehow. The tingling sensation turned into sparks that shot through her, creating a series of little tremors.

"Not yet."

"Can I see it?"

"It's very cloudy out."

"But I could still see that it's daylight?"

"From the east tower. I've a grand view of the estate from there."

"Oh! Sweet! You're thinking of a tour?"

Munson interrupted from somewhere in the vicinity. Rachel barely heard it. She placed her hand within Wystan's. He lifted it to his lips, without releasing her rapt gaze. He touched a kiss to her knuckles, and her heart flipped. Or something close. She imagined she was floating, encapsulated in light. Wonder. Joy. Behind her, Munson sighed. The sound contained a bit of awe with it.

Someone cleared their throat in the hall beyond Wystan.

The instant it happened, the bubble of bliss about her popped. Rachel dropped, as if she'd actually been hovering above the tiled floor. The landing jolted slightly. But that was ridiculous. Nothing could alter reality that much. And surely Munson would've noticed.

"Begging pardon, Sir, but a car has arrived."

"A car?"

Wystan lowered her hand and turned his head slightly to ask it. He didn't release her gaze or her hand. He laced his fingers through hers, holding her hand against his side. And she helped.

"Oh. Hello again, Roderick."

Eleanor came around Rachel. She hadn't noticed how they'd blocked the entrance to the room. She hadn't noticed anything. Other than Wystan. And what he made her feel.

"Well. That's that. No tour for me. Looks like I'm heading back to London. Got a flight to catch. So. Rachel? You...uh...coming with me? Or not?"

Wystan tensed. His fingers tightened against hers. And his eyes grew blacker. Those were physical signs that he cared about her answer, while something indefinable heightened the air about them. Something virile. Dangerous. And endlessly exciting. He wasn't even breathing.

"I don't know," Rachel replied. "Anything I say...would sound like I'm angling for an invitation."

Wystan lifted their conjoined hands to his lips again. "Oh, no. No. Please. Stay with me. Please?"

Her heart did crazy palpitations within her breast. The bra might be the right size, but it felt like a rubber band around her ribs at the moment and twice as constrictive. She'd never seen such a look. Oh, why was she even hesitating?

"Well. That looks like an invitation to me, Berne. What do you say? Long flight home...or a bit of vacation touring this place? Time's wasting and I'm probably burning petrol out there. I do love these Brit terms. Loo. Petrol. Chips."

Rachel barely heard Munson's chatting over the incessant tones filling her ear. It was like a blending of notes, all in the tenor range. Rachel stepped the tiniest space closer to Wystan.

"You'll show me the sunset first? Right now?"

Wystan's lip twitched as if he hid a smile. He pulled her closer by tucking their conjoined hands against his chest. "Most assuredly," he replied.

"All right."

Rachel didn't even feel her lips agreeing, but it was her voice. The waves of tension she'd felt coming off of Wystan altered almost instantly. They evaporated as he closed his eyes, put his head back, and something akin to a sigh came from him.

Was it truly possible that she mattered so much to him?

"Well then. That's that. Looks like I'm traveling solo. Roderick? Lead the way, buddy."

Munson's voice came cheerfully, breaking the spell. Then, the woman was gone and the entire world filled with Wystan. She watched as he lowered his head, snagged her gaze again, and sent her heart stuttering. All of it improbable. Impossible. And incredible.

She couldn't possibly feel anything for this man. No. She didn't. They barely knew each other.

"Hold tight."

"What?"

"We've little time before the sun sets. And the tower is some distance, my love."

"Please don't call me that," she replied.

"What?"

"Um...love."

He chuckled and started moving. Rachel hung on. Images flashed before her eyes. A maze of halls. A myriad of doors. Rooms. Weapons displays. Suits of armor. Fireplaces. Tapestry-covered walls. More halls, some painted with a white finish that glowed, others covered with wooden paneling that sucked up the light. Nowhere could she spot a window, although he had some sort of electrical lighting system. And all sorts of museum-quality furnishings. She couldn't tell, for certain. They were moving too fast. As it they didn't even need steps.

Then even the lighting altered.

They entered a supremely old section of the castle, or her eyes were deceiving her. It could be a set for some sword and sorcery movie with its solid stone walls and high arched ceilings. She couldn't make out height. They moved too quickly, and it was too dark. Any illumination came from torchlight. They passed each torch cresset at a speed that caused the flames to sputter. Wystan snagged one as they flew past. She knew why once they entered a well of space too wide to see the dimension. They were at the base of a spiral stone staircase. It was an immense structure that wrapped about a center pillar of more stone.

"The east tower wheel-stair."

Wystan said it, although she hadn't asked. His voice echoed weirdly up the stairs, giving the impression of space. Height. Volume. She'd seen this sort of thing in books. She'd never imagined actually climbing one.

She gripped Wystan's hand a bit tighter, and grabbed his arm with her free hand as he started up the steps. She couldn't tell how many steps he climbed, or how many floors they passed. She kept her eyes on him, ignoring the whorl of stone about them that confused and dazed. Her senses should have been reeling. They weren't. She actually felt like she was vibrating.

The steps ended at a landing of more stone, backed by a large, unadorned wooden door. With what looked like ancient hinges. An enormous plank of wood was across it, bolting it shut. Wystan lifted the bolt with his free hand, secured it into a hook on the side, and pulled the door open.

Fresh air assailed her. It carried a chill. A light sprinkling of snowflakes. And a brisk breeze that blew out the torch almost instantly. They didn't need the light. It was definitely late afternoon. Even with the cloud cover she had no trouble seeing Wystan. The breeze pulled some of his hair loose from his queue. He truly was gorgeous. Massive. Strong.

And like nothing dead.

The sudden squeezing sensation about her heart was almost painful. Rachel sucked in a breath with surprise. It wasn't remotely possible. Or probable. Or even plausible. She'd just met him. She wasn't even sure there was such a thing as love anymore. She'd seen too much. Experienced worse. She couldn't possibly be feeling anything like love. Not this soon.

He stepped toward the stone encircling the parapet, taking her with him. Rachel wasn't fond of heights, but she didn't feel remotely scared. Emotions long dormant, took over. She was young. Unfettered. Slightly giddy. And the view was breath-taking. In any direction. Rachel swiveled in place, trying to take it all in. Wystan turned with her, always at her side. His fingers still locked to hers, holding her close. She'd never considered holding hands to be so heart-warming.

It just was.

There was a lot of light in one section, blooming over a huge wall. That was probably the faire. Dark spots interspersed the grounds. They might be forested areas. She could make out headlights piercing the gloom. That could be Munson's car. It was just beyond the outer wall. Rachel counted three of the huge stone walls encircling the grounds. The sight was magnificent.

"How...high are we?" she asked.

"Thirty meters. Maybe."

"Seriously? How many stories does this place have?"

He grinned, highlighting the little laugh lines about his eyes. What light there was glinted off his perfect teeth. Nothing out-of-order. No fangs. No pallor. Nothing paranormal. Nothing vampiric. Anywhere.

"I don't know for certain. Some parts of the castle have four levels. Some five. Others only two. Construction was ongoing for centuries, using various stone masons. Not much is exactly square. Some of the doorjambs are off-kilter. The doors fit, but they slant. It's rather entertaining."

"It's an amazing view." She shivered.

"You cold, my love?"

He dropped her hand and had her wrapped in his jacket almost before he'd finished asking. Rachel snuggled into it, getting warmed. Enwrapped. Captivated. And then she steeled herself to ignore it.

"I asked you not to call me that, Wystan."

"Oh. Yes. You did. Apologies."

He grinned. She didn't return it.

"Um...listen. Before we go any further, I need to...thank you."

"Thank me?"

"For showing me daylight. Specifically...for showing me how you look in it."

"Pardon?"

"Oh, you heard me. I don't know you very well, Wystan, but I think I might like to. I mean, I had a really great time uh...last night. I mean this morning. With you. Um...in bed. But I have to tell you. That was an anomaly. I'm not that easy. I was really close to leaving before you showed me this." She gestured toward the sky.

"I do not understand."

"Look. Wystan. If we're going to take this to another level, we have to clear the air."

"We do?"

"Sex is one thing. And if that's all you're looking for, well. You might as well just keep looking."

He chuckled and his eyes warmed somehow. And that was ridiculous.

"You are so...young."

Rachel's lips tightened. "Look. I'm almost thirty. And age has nothing to do with it. I'm a cop. We don't trust easily. We don't like subterfuge and lies. We get hives when we're confronted with nut cases. And we *really* detest frauds."

"If this is related to me, I could take offence."

"Oh. It's related to you. And, if that bothers you, well. Sorry. It's about to get more offensive."

"I do not understand."

"You want it in black and white? You got it." She took a deep breath. "You are not a vampire."

His lips twitched as if he were hiding a smile. "Truly?"

"They don't exist. And, even if I suspended reality and believed it, that bit of daylight right there, is a dead giveaway. Excuse the pun. So. That means you're either a nut case. Or you lied to me...and you're a fraud."

"You're shivering," he replied.

"Well. The sun is setting, it's cold out here, and you're avoiding answering. Maybe I should call for a ride, too."

"My lady, please? I...have words that need to be said. There is so much to speak of. So much to show you. I did not plan on doing it here."

"Why not?"

"You wish a declaration out here?"

A declaration?

"Um. Wystan. We need to talk."

"Yes. I know. But not here."

He looked down at her for long moments, and then he smiled. Her heart flipped. She felt it.

"Come. Take my hand. I'll explain everything. I promise."

Rachel hesitated to a full count of three. Then, she gave him her hand. And then he leapt right over the edge of the parapet with her.

CHAPTER ELEVEN

Wystan swooped through the snow-flecked air, landing lithely on a second-floor balcony. Rachel had gasped when they'd first jumped, but then she'd gone silent. She also burrowed against him, her head just beneath his chin. She gripped tightly to the hand she held, while her other arm wrapped about his ribcage. The embrace was doing all sorts of things to him. Exhilarating. Energizing. Exciting.

His teeth tingled while shivers roamed his flesh. He had to calm this. He couldn't make love to her again. Not yet. Not until she knew and accepted. Yet, despite his sense of honor and chivalry, he wasn't at all sure he could keep from changing her. Her blood called to his. Her very essence pulled at him. He had to calm this! He mustn't scare her. Wystan walked from the balcony into a hall, shutting the door behind him and sealing out the elements.

"You all right, love?" he whispered against her hair.

"We just jumped...off the roof!"

Her voice was shaky. It matched her entire frame. He tightened his arm about her and kept walking.

The east tower was attached to the original keep, the oldest section of the castle. It was begun during William the Conqueror's reign, to subdue Welsh tribes. The strongest lords had been settled in each castle. Wystan's grand-father had been one of them, but he'd gone a step further. He'd married a Welsh princess, blending Celtic traditions with Norman. Celt heritage was the meaning behind Wystan's middle name as well as the shading of his VAL tattoo.

Wystan entered a newer section, added in the fifteenth century. This addition coincided with the founding of the College of Arms. Wystan had wanted a stone edifice, with barrel-vaulted ceilings and thick, stone pillars, to house and display his Order of Honor garter, the *de* Crecy shield, coat-of-arms, banner, his tournament and battle armor, and other regalia. The area was perfectly maintained. The displays dusted, the armor polished. There would be one candle lit at all times. Overseeing that fell to the *de* Crecy Sergeant-At-Arms. Wystan had gone through eleven of them. All loyal, responsible men. The latest rendition was approaching seventy. He was hard of hearing, slow and stooped, and hopefully busy eating his sup.

Access was either from the front portal outside, or through this hall. Wystan had guessed right. No one halted him as they neared. Rachel clung tighter, however. It was a problem. Wystan concentrated on the words he was about to speak. It didn't help much. Her frame was too luscious, and the mate bond too strong. He groaned softly.

They reached a large, engraved door. Wystan opened it with his free hand and walked in, shutting it behind him. He'd used too much power. The sound boomed through the room. He'd been off a bit. This Sergeant-At-Arms had the archival candle lit, and several torches as well. That was fortuitous. Shadows flit all about the displays, while light glinted off armor, swords, and glass cases. Wystan walked toward a large bench placed in the center of a spiral the tile-layers had designed into the floor.

They reached the bench. Wystan stood for a moment. She felt so wondrous in his arms. He smiled down at her.

"I'm going to set you down now. You ready?"

She nodded, and disengaged her arm from about him as he moved her. She looked incongruous in her pink fur hat, matching slacks, and his over-sized dark jacket. And she looked just right at the same time. He waited as she settled atop the blue cushion. And then he went to his knees, putting his face just below hers.

"You are so lucky the rope held," she told him.

"What rope?"

"The one you used for your leap. And I have to tell you. You're good. I almost believed it."

"Rachel."

"You're also lucky I'm not the type to sue. Or whatever the English call it. I mean, if you're going to take people on death-defying stunts, you need to get written permission beforehand. Then again, it would have ruined your little surprise. And I almost believed it. Almost."

Akron had told him this might get complicated.

That was an understatement.

Wystan cleared his throat. "Have you ever heard of heraldry?"

"Um. Maybe. What is it?"

"It is a term encasing family pedigree, titles, arms, recording honors, assigning a place in society. All of that."

Her eyebrows rose and her head tipped just slightly. He didn't know what that meant. So, he kept talking.

"It starts with a coat of arms design. The *de* Crecy family goes back to the Norman Conquest. Coats of arms followed in the thirteenth century. There are rules that had to be followed, called *blazon*. They're very strict. For instance, you can only use two of three materials; colors, metals, or fur. And once the design is in place, only the titleholder can use it in the pure form. A cousin, or other member of the family, may have the same coat of arms, but it must be altered with a border or different background. This alteration is called a mark of cadency, or *brisure*. The *de* Crecy design is a silver field with a standing blue dragon in the center. It's on my shield and all the banners. The technical name is '*argent* a dragon *rampant d'azure*'. It translates literally to silver dragon standing on blue."

"Why is it in French?"

"The entire court was Norman French until the Tudor Royal House was founded in 1485. The oath of the Honor Garter is still taken in French. To this day."

"You're not serious, are you?"

"Hear me out. Please?"

She gave a heavy sigh. He was boring her? Wystan moved to wrap his other hand about the one he held, and then he told her.

"I speak of the Honor Garter for a reason, Rachel. It is a rare honor, bestowed by the monarch, for valor and bravery in battle. I earned mine in 1346."

"I hope you're not trying to impress me, because where I come from, nobody cares about this kind of stuff. A man is respected not for who his parents are, but what he is. And what he does. And what he makes of himself. It's called integrity."

"You didn't listen, my love. I'm telling you that *I* earned the Honor Garter. In the year 1346."

"I heard that part, and I'm still telling you—. Did you just say *you* earned it?"

He nodded.

"Oh. Come on, Wystan. First the jump stunt and then this? And...darn. I was thinking we really might create something together."

"There's more," he replied.

"Oh. This should be good. Okay. Hit me with it."

"I did not lie to you. I am not a fraud. And I am not a nut case."

"And you're several hundred years old, too. Right. Got it. I think I'll call for a pick-up now. You get reception in here?"

She pulled a cell phone from somewhere beneath his coat and her jacket. He watched as she touched a button.

"I am a vampire, Rachel Berne."

He used the full range of his voice. It rattled armament throughout the room. A sword fell somewhere in the dimness as if for emphasis. The phone dropped into her lap.

"Holy crap, Wystan!"

"I swear it to you, Rachel. I am a vampire. I accepted vampirism over death in the year 1349. It was an easy choice. I fell from my horse during a battle and took a lance in the side. My *destrier* died. I didn't."

"No way."

He flashed to the fallen sword and returned before she managed to retrieve her phone. He placed the blade across his knees, gripping the hilt in his right hand as he watched her.

Good.

It was one of the newer blades. Purely ceremonial. Fairly short. Less than a meter in length. She was shaking. Her grip on her phone looked questionable. Her eyes were wide, too. She had stunning eyes. Silver. If she wore *de* Crecy colors, she'd be impossible to overlook. Visually stunning. He should have known.

"How do you move that quickly?"

"I'm a vampire, love. It comes with certain...abilities. Speed. Strength. Vision."

"No. No. Vampires are not real."

She shook her head. He grinned.

"I am real," he repeated. "And I am a vampire. Here. I'll attempt to prove it to you again."

He turned the sword and sliced a deep cut in his left arm from elbow to wrist. His sweater threads turned bloody as they separated. Her cry of shock accompanied it.

And...merde!.

Wystan winced even as the cut started closing. He'd forgotten what pain felt like. He dropped the sword to the floor and shoved his sleeve up. She didn't say a thing as the cut closed, and then sealed, and then disappeared. She didn't appear to be breathing. And she was starting to sway on her stool.

"You're not going to faint, are you?" Wystan asked.

She put both hands to the sides of her hips and steadied herself. And then she narrowed her eyes.

"Nice try, Wystan. Really. That was gory. But...I'm still not buying it. They use props like that in the movies. It's extremely lifelike. I've heard of it. I've just never seen it. But I've heard of it."

"You are difficult to convince, my love. Wait. I have it. I will be right back."

Wystan zipped to a suit of armor. Fifteenth century. He grabbed the *cuirass*. He didn't care that the rest of the suit fell. He only needed the breastplate. He'd chosen well. This one was unornamented. Shiny. Reflective. He sat beside her on the bench and held it out. He could easily see her reflection. His was missing.

"Here. Look. Vampires cast no shadows and we don't have a reflection. Go ahead. Look for yourself."

She looked. And then she stared. She grabbed the *cuirass* and worked it back and forth, trying to find his image. And then she turned to him.

"You don't have a reflection, Wystan."

"I know. I told you."

"This is impossible."

The *cuirass* dropped to the floor, making the room ring with the sound of steel against tile for several moments.

"Do you believe me now?"

"I...don't know."

"What? What more do you need?"

Wystan's breath hitched. His throat tightened oddly. A shiver ran along all his back. Legs. Arms. He wrapped his hands into fists and then tightened them until the knuckles turned white. Was nothing going to convince her? What else could he do? *What?* He'd never come up against such skepticism and disbelief. It was doubly worse because it mattered so much!

"Give me a minute, okay? I came to England to catch a pervert. I didn't come here to have the fabric of physics blasted apart. It just *isn't* possible."

"But...you do believe me?"

"Wystan. If you're a real vampire, then my entire belief system has just been shot to smithereens. I mean, come on. I'm a right-brained person. Logical. Scientific. I don't believe in supernatural stuff. Aliens. Werewolves. Ghosts. Vampires. They're figments of somebody's fertile imagination. Or a junkie's best friend. They're not real. I can't possibly believe in them. I'd get laughed out of the precinct."

"Even if it's true?"

"Especially if it's true. There isn't a drug around to alter this. I mean, if I believe in vampires...what's next? Huh? Where does it end?"

"You ready?"

"For what?"

"What's next."

"Oh, no. You mean...there's *more*?"

Her eyes went wide, showing the dark-toned blue about the edges. The perfect fringe of lash she had about them. If Wystan wasn't already fully hooked, that look would have snagged, caught, and then secured him.

He swiveled, moving from sitting at her side to kneeling at her feet again. He forced his hands from their fisted shapes before reaching them out toward her, palms upward. He held that position for countless moments, holding his breath, and feeling an emotion that might actually be fear. And finally she responded, placing her hands within his. The relief was palpable. Intense. But her fingers were icy. And she was visibly shaking.

"I have been a vampire for centuries, Rachel Berne. Centuries. It isn't anything like what the storytellers portray. Vampirism is not eternal life. It is eternal death. I had no feelings. No emotions. No passions. No sensation. No...uh...ability to love a woman, if you understand what I am trying to say."

"Now you're going to tell me I imagined...that lovemaking session?"

"Oh no. No. Rachel. That was real. And perfect. Well beyond anything I have ever experienced. Ever." Wystan pulled in a large breath, expanding his chest before exhaling with a heavy sigh. "This is not working. I'll try explaining another way. Have you ever heard of soul mates?"

Her eyes went even wider.

"You have? You've heard of soul-mates? Two beings destined for each other? Regardless of time and physical restraints? Regardless even...of death? You have heard of that?"

"That's another...bit of fiction, Wystan. Studies have proven the ability to love more than one person in a lifetime."

"I'm not talking about just love!"

He didn't control his voice. More armor fell in the room about them. She pulled her hands free and covered her face with them. And he'd promised not to scare her!

"Rachel, please? Forgive my outburst. I'll try to control it better. It's just—! I'm just—! Ah!"

Wystan arched backwards and let the emotion out. That was stupid. A thud resounded through the room as something heavy fell, and two of the torches blew out. She was still hiding behind her hands when he looked back at her. He was failing at chivalrous behavior, too. The one thing a knight would never do was accost and frighten a lady.

He swallowed.

"My lady. Please. I...am speaking so poorly, because it means so much to me. I will try and be more succinct and less emotional. Please say you forgive me and will listen still. Please?"

She nodded. She didn't move her hands. It was the only sign she gave. It would have to be enough. He didn't know what to do, so he started talking again.

"You mention love, and—oh! I don't know. When I was alive before, they spoke of courtly love. Such a love was supposed to transcend physical lust. It didn't seem real. It seemed overly-dramatic and false...a way for a knight to get a lady's favor in a joust. Perhaps curry support with a powerful lord. I couldn't help hearing about it, though. Troubadours sang for hours on the subject. I never experienced it. Perhaps one can love more than once in a lifetime. I don't know.

"That isn't a mate, Rachel. I'm speaking of soul-mates. It's not just love. It is so much more. A mate-bond is something that can reach through an eternity of lifelessness and kick a dead heart back to life. It is that powerful. I was told about it when I was first changed. I didn't believe. It didn't exist. It was a dream. It wasn't real. For centuries of time I was right. And then...things changed. The moment you drew near, my heart started beating again. My emotions returned. My passions. My...ah! I still can't explain. My entire world has been upended. All I know is, I have a mate. And I found her. You."

She pulled her hands down, covering her mouth with her fingers while she regarded him.

"What else can I say? What shall I do? Don't...you feel it, too?"

As he watched, her eyes went wet. Shiny. Looking exactly like polished silver.

I made her cry? No. Oh, no.

"Please don't cry, my love."

She sniffed, blinked, and a solitary tear dropped onto her cheek. A swell of emotion slammed through him. It electrified, and it terrified. Now, Wystan was trembling.

"Forgive me. I went too fast."

She shook her head.

"I didn't go fast enough?"

"I don't know...what to say," she told him.

"Say that you feel it, too. You have to! You must! Maybe not when we first met, but surely you felt it later...when we joined? I have never felt such wonder, Rachel Berne. Please say you felt it, too? Something? Anything?"

"Wystan. Please."

His newly-awakened heart kept pumping, sending something heavy and painful with each beat.

"Rachel. Look me in the eye and tell me you don't feel anything for me."

"We...just met."

"Yes. We did. But time is meaningless. When you've existed for enough of it, you learn that. Yes, we just met. And yes, I am going too fast. But I don't know any other way! What else I can say? I used to think I had nothing but time. Now it feels like I've got seconds to convince you of what you mean to me. I've never had a mate. I'll never have another. You are everything to me, Rachel Berne. Everything. My future. My life. My joy."

"Wystan?"

She didn't sound convinced. She sounded impossibly young, and immeasurably unsure. And slightly frightened. Wystan bowed his head and shook with what couldn't possibly be sobs. No. Never. Not a knight of the Honor Garter. His eyes burned. A knot formed in his throat, making an obstruction he had to swallow around. It wasn't possible. He'd failed? And now, he was ready to cry?

Wystan raced to a lance and brought it back. He'd moved so quickly, she still had her hands atop her mouth and the exact same look on her face. He had to blink rapidly in order to see. And then look away just as quickly. He couldn't tell what her expression signified. Horror?

He spoke to the span of room on his right.

"Rachel Berne. You are my mate. My one...and my only. I love you. I do not lie. I am not a fraud. And I am not remotely insane. I am simply a vampire who has found his mate. But it is supposed to be a wondrous thing, not a pain beyond comprehension."

"What are you doing, Wystan?"

He swallowed. The knot shifted. It made his voice gruff. "There are two certain ways to kill a vampire, Rachel. Sunlight is not one of them. That only works with the newly created."

"So, that's why it failed."

He nodded. He didn't dare look up at her. His heart was a solid throb of agony, sending pain with every continued beat. He didn't know what might happen if he looked at her. He might do something completely ignoble and burst into sobs. It was an actual possibility that alarmed and panicked. And those emotions he'd never dealt with before.

"One...method is to slice the head off." His body shuddered with emotion he couldn't suppress. His voice betrayed him, too, as each word trembled. He lifted the lance and even it shook visibly. "The other method is well known. It's a wooden stake, shoved right through the heart."

Wystan smacked a fist into the lance. It broke, leaving two uneven ends. He tossed the one with the spike over his shoulder. It hit something breakable. He heard glass shatter and more sounds of items falling. He didn't care what it was. Not anymore. He ran a thumb over the end of the section he still held. It was jagged, but not quite sharp enough. He picked up the sword and started carving, using brutal swift strokes that whittled the end to a spike.

"Wystan? What...are you doing?"

There.

The stake looked just about perfect. Wystan looked up at her. Blinked her into focus. And then looked away.

"I need you to make a call now, my lady."

"A...call?"

"Yes."

"Who am I calling?"

"It won't matter. Your friend Munson will do. Tell her about me. Be sure to speak of a vampire. Tell her my history. Exactly as I told you. Stay on the line for at least forty-one seconds. Longer, if possible."

"Why forty-one seconds?"

"I've been told that is enough time to find a signal and trace it. And after the call, I need you to leave. Hide somewhere. Or...I suppose you can stay and watch."

"Watch...for what?"

"Hunters. They've got a camp near the coast. They think it's hidden. Or, they may send a group from Manchester. That's their base."

"Hunters?"

"Yes."

"There's such a thing as a vampire hunter, too?"

Wystan nodded.

"So...why did you make a stake for them?"

"They're fairly inept. I'm assisting."

"You're serious, aren't you?'

"Make the call, Rachel."

Wystan bowed his head and waited, alert to the sound of her pushing buttons. Instead he got the sound of more glass shattering. And then a lot of tinkling sounds. He looked up in time to watch Rachel move off the cushion and join him on the floor. She took the stake from his nerveless fingers and chucked it, too.

She didn't hit anything other than a wall. Wystan was frowning as the sound of a rolling stick finally stopped. She dusted her hands together, using exaggerated broad strokes and then she planted them on her knees.

"What...are you doing?" he asked.

"Taking a turn."

She tipped her chin up and then she smiled. Wystan blinked rapidly several times. Her expression didn't change.

"At what?"

"Breaking stuff."

"Why?"

She shrugged. "Looked like fun. And I had to get that stake away from you somehow...now, didn't I?"

"Uh...Rachel?"

"Besides...I think this place is a bit archaic. You know..." she wrinkled her nose. "Old. It really could use a woman's touch. Just as long as you don't expect me to clean up the mess, anyway."

She scooted closer. Wystan watched her. He was afraid to move. Breathe. Think. Hope was a very scary thing at the moment.

"Do you understand what I'm saying, Sir Wystan Ryn *de* Crecy? Or do I need to get more specific?"

"Um..."

"You're really kind of cute with that confused look on your face. Oh. What am I saying? You're always cute. And yes, I feel something pretty powerful. And yes. I could very easily admit to loving you. But no. I'm not exactly sold on this vampire thing...but if it's at all like last night—whoa! You can fly, too?"

He'd seized her up and held her. Close to his heart. Her arms were locked about his shoulders. Her legs wrapped about his hips.

She called this flying?

It was more like soaring.

And if the *de* Crecy banners hadn't stopped him, he'd have probably slammed right through the stone vaulted ceiling.

And he wouldn't have cared about that, either.

-o0o-

A Vampire Assassin League Novella

ANYONE HERE

JACKIE IVIE

CHAPTER ONE

"Your left! There's one on your left! He's going to—!"

"Calm down, Nigel, boy. Look to your own laurels. I've got it well in hand. You see?"

The answer was serious and calm, the complete opposite of the original speaker. But then the calmness got overridden by a high-five smacking celebratory sound of palm to palm as gore splattered the large screen. Even as it dissipated, more black-clothed figures joined the fight, swords swinging, limbs flying, and that got both players back to their controllers, moving buttons, pushing levers, and calling taunts toward one another.

"There's more than one way to skin a cat. Watch this!"

"Skin a cat?"

"You need to get out more, Crusader. A lot more. See?"

"See what?"

A figure went flying across one half of the split screen, landing in a heap that dissolved into a puddle, and then even that dried up and disappeared. Before it was gone, another landed in the exact spot, gaining hoots and cheers from both men.

"Come on, Akron. Surely you're not serious. You summoned me all the way from sunny California to watch The Crusader and Nigel playing a video game?"

"Oh. It's not just any game, Len. It's the latest thing. Called *Bellus*."

"*Bellus*?"

"Latin word. Means war. And wait. There's a *Daemon Bellus* level. Nigel has about reached it."

"Not without me, he doesn't," Invaris grumbled.

"*Bellus*. Hmm…interesting," Len replied.

"Not just interesting. Popular. Or in the current lingo – virulent. Debuted last weekend and is already gaining massive devotees. By the minute. See that little number scale on the lower left there?"

Little was a misnomer. Since they were watching the play on a 120 inch LED screen, the numbers were almost a foot high.

"Yes."

"It changes every fifteen minutes. Getting higher and higher. That's how many players are online playing *Bellus* right now. As we speak. It's the newest craze. Notice anything…else?"

"It's in a castle."

"True. Most of the activity takes place either in a castle or on the grounds directly outside. You should see the crypt and the cemetery levels. Anything else?"

"The players are hidden. Nobody has a face."

"Very good. That's only in the beginning. You need to go immortal to get a personalized avatar with recognizable features."

A dull throb of sound hit the speakers, sounding a bit like an old brass bell atop a belfry.

"Oh good. Nigel has just reached immortal status. Invaris?"

Another gong sound throbbed through the room, bouncing off the stone walls of what went for a media room in the Vampire Assassin League's headquarters.

"Right behind him, Sir."

"Just remember that, Crusader. You're behind."

"By three whole players. Just look. Out of the three million-plus players, I'm number 68,308 in rankings. And I started this evening. You played all last night."

"You're still behind," Nigel fired back.

"Just pick your avatars, gentlemen. You can fight with them on the screen. Here is where it gets interesting, Len. Watch closely now. This is why I summoned you."

A box opened in the center of each side of the screen, listing all sorts of immortal beings. Gargoyles. Werewolves. Demons. Vampires. Trolls. Angels. Fairies. Dragons. Aliens. As the players ran their cursers over the listings, the words lit up. Both men ended up choosing vampire. Len smirked.

"You picking the Viking again?" Nigel asked.

"Of course."

"Me too. He's got the most power."

"Just for that, Nigel, you're going to select the Rus." Akron informed him.

"Oh come on. A woman?"

"She's got a special skill-set. Rips out hearts with the flick of her wrist. As well as other body parts."

"I'd rather be the Hun."

"Pick him, then."

Nigel sighed loudly. "Why can't I be Dane, too? He's the best one."

"Dane?" Len choked out.

"Starting to look a bit more familiar, is it?" Akron asked.

"I don't believe this," Len replied.

"Continue on, gentlemen. We're waiting."

A thick-muscled Viking avatar lit up Invaris's side of the screen. A large, fur-covered fellow showed up on Nigel's, holding the distinctive backward-curving bow for which the Huns were known. A moment later both avatars were racing along a dark stone-enclosed corridor, not unlike the VAL's own halls.

"Doesn't the Viking get a weapon?" Len asked.

"Oh…he'll pick them up as he goes. But, Nigel found the real clue to Dane's power sometime this morning. It's the reason they're both so high in the statistics and moving upward with every win."

"How?"

"Once the Viking avatar finds and inserts an arm into a special slit in the wall – no bigger than a slice of light – he gets to go into Berserker mode. And that's all he really needs."

"What? Berserker mode?" Len was on his feet and glaring at the screen.

"And with that comes the ability to rip limbs off, slam opponents through walls, stuff like that.

Everything sent at him bounces off. I'd say he's pretty much invincible."

"That's why I wanted him, too," Nigel complained.

Gore splattered across the screen, a disembodied arm at the center. Then a torso. Len turned away and walked over to Akron's desk. Sat down. Picked at a nonexistent piece of lint on his jacket. And then lifted his gaze to his boss.

"Babycakes really owes me this time," he said.

"Truly?"

"That was my idea. Mine."

"So…you did say this would make a good video game?"

"Right. And that jackass went and stole it. As if he needs the money. You better tell him I'm going to want my half. Screw that. I want 75 percent and not one penny less."

"You don't know anything about this?"

"Hell no. But I'm getting more pissed the longer I do know about it."

"You didn't design a video game, copyright it, and then market it?"

"With what time? I'm on your team. I spend my time training, working out, familiarizing and then excelling at all sorts of weaponry. Otherwise, I wouldn't be very good at my job. Video games are for the sedentary, not for guys like me."

"You didn't pay someone to do it, then?"

"I'm going to hazard a guess you've already checked my accounts. Does it look like I've recently got a massive infusion of capital?"

"Damn it! I hate this stinkin' Hun! He makes a lousy vampire! Always did. About the only thing he's good for is bashing heads. And you have to get close enough for that. I get close and—shit! Look at that. Now I have to re-spawn and go back to mortality." Nigel complained loudly, shoving back into his seat.

"You should use the bow. That's what it's for."

"Stow it, Crusader Man. You just watch your back. Or whatever. Berserker mode only lasts three minutes, and then you'll be just like me again."

"Except I'll be above you on the charts."

"Bastard."

"Whiner."

"Gentlemen. Please. I'm trying to have a conversation here with our compatriot, Leonard. I'm going to be unplugging the set in a moment. And I never thought I'd say that combination of words. I sound like the father of teenagers."

Both men went silent and returned to flicking buttons, while their bodies followed every move. Len watched them for a moment and then turned back. "How much is Babycakes making on this?"

"Dane is on his honeymoon. Still. He isn't designing video games. I checked the moment Nigel found the Berserker Mode this morning. And then I called you."

"Don't believe it."

"Trust me. Dane is in the middle of the Arctic Ocean, ice-locked for the most part. I've verified it. He hasn't had contact with the real world for months. His Key West bars are even for sale. I don't think he misses any of it."

"Sounds like a really nice honeymoon," Len said in a sarcastic tone. It was completely wasted on his employer.

"No doubt. Lots of cold, but that doesn't worry a member of the undead. And let's not forget. It's dark up there...especially this time of year. Pitch dark is always good, especially for a new vampire like Evangeline."

"If Dane Monroe didn't design that damn game...who did? And how did they know?"

"Good question. But I believe he's going by Morgan this time around."

"Like I care! I want names and I want them now. You have access. Get one of your boys to find me some names and addresses. I'll handle the rest."

Akron was punching keys on his laptop. "Already on it. I just had to make certain you weren't involved. Always check the simplest option before moving on. That's the cornerstone of good puzzle-solving, you know."

"Me? You really think I'm stupid? I work for you - the most elite firm in the world. And I know anyone betraying V.A.L. is a dead man. A real dead man. V.A.L. can find an insect carcass in the middle of the Amazon jungle. They can find my ass."

"Money is a great motivator. Turns even the smartest into fools...and this little video game is making a lot of money."

"Money is just green paper. Honor and trust are what matter. You have mine. Still. Always."

"Well...you know me, Len. I had to check. There! Well hidden behind two LLCs and more than one alias, but not hidden well enough. I've found you, Jonas...no. Make that Jacob. Jacob Walsh. Jake. Sounds like an Irish street fighter, doesn't he? No picture? That's odd."

"Give me his address. I'll handle his demise. Gratis."

"Ah! Finally! There's a picture. From an old equity article, published when he was at MIT. Jacob Walsh appears to be the new breed – a self-made man. With lots of brains, ready cash, and reams of so-called friends. Hard to get close to. Harder to photograph. But look. He appears to like the ladies. Lots and lots of them, if this write-up is correct. I know the perfect operative. Jake? You are about to be baited, hooked, and then reeled in. And then maybe I'll fillet you. Invaris?"

"Sir."

The knight stood and dropped his controller into his chair seat, leaving his avatar standing in the midst of a melee of blood and flame. Nigel's Hun came striding through the midst of it, and slammed the Viking backwards.

"Call up Cassandra Braun. She's been dormant since that riot in the 60s."

"On it, Sir." The Crusader walked toward the door.

"Check London. If I don't miss my guess, she's still hunting around the cemetery near Highgate."

"A Brit?" Len asked.

"More than a Brit. A Victorian. You ever hear of the Industrial Revolution?" Akron asked.

"Oh please. Do I look like I just parachuted onto this planet?"

"Good thing I like you, Leonard. That's all I'm going to say about your sarcasm. Cassandra is a product of her time. A Victorian woman hailing from White Chapel district. I think she might even know the real identity of Jack the Ripper, though she won't tell."

"Can't wait to meet her. When do I leave?"

"Not yet. You've got another job. In Texas. Excuse me a moment, Len. Nigel! Stop that. It's bad form."

"What?" Nigel's Hun stopped stomping up and down on Invaris's Viking, mainly due to having the fingers controlling the avatar finally stilled. Nigel stood and looked over at Akron.

"I really wonder if you're ever going to grow up," Akron commented, to no one in particular. And then he disappeared.

CHAPTER TWO

Sixty- seven. Sixty- eight. Sixty—

Jake's fingers touched the pad, stopping the timer. In a flash he was shoving up from the water, wiping moisture from his eyes, and grinning. Widely. That was followed by a yelp of exaltation as he slapped at the water. Outstanding! He'd bettered his time by four one-hundredths of a second and used two less strokes to do it! He'd verify with video later, but it felt and looked like he'd not only beat his personal best, but elongated his stroke as well. If he kept this up, he might try out for the Olympic team again. That should shock the hell out of everyone.

"You stayin' in there all night, Love?"

Jake swiveled, putting his back against the pool edge in order to look over and then up. There was a woman poised nonchalantly at the side of his pool. A woman. In his house. Right beside his pool, for crap sake. With him wearing only sharkskin trunks for defense. He didn't know what he paid security guards for.

It was difficult to see her face through the nose-grazing length of black lace falling from her hat. Or what might pass for a hat if it was larger than three square inches in size. It sat atop a mass of dark red curls as if somehow holding all her coiffure from falling to her butt. Or maybe that mane was even thigh-length. She wasn't looking at him. She was swirling the long pointed end of a slender umbrella in his pool, twirling little whirlpools into existence.

Jake sloshed his free hand over his face again, swiping water away, before narrowing his eyes. It didn't work. There was still a woman standing there, dressed in something more fitted to a Halloween party. He'd rank it steam-punk only it put everything he'd ever seen to shame. And she didn't disappear.

She turned her head and sent a glance at him. A rush of flame roared through his chest, ratcheting his heartbeat higher than his swim had. *Whoa Jacob.* She had intense cobalt blue eyes. Even through the black lace curtain falling from her hat, nobody could miss that color, or those eyes. And from what he could see, she was jaw-dropping gorgeous. Sinfully so. More so than the cadre of swimsuit models his friends had assembled for his party in Cabo San Lucas last month…the same party that had bored him within three days. And then disgusted. All parties anymore seemed to have the same trouble. Maybe he was getting old.

Nah. Twenty-eight isn't old, Jake. It's just right. He had the world at his feet. Women were available twenty-four-seven. Clothing optional. He was just sated. Jaded. Bored. That's why he'd gone on an abstinence diet from feminine companionship for at least a month. And then look at what happens? A babe dressed as a late Victorian-era vamp just appears. And as he'd instantly noted, she was more gorgeous than any swimsuit model. Shapelier, too. A lot shapelier. Her bosom warranted more than a glance. It looked real, too, as if no plastic surgeon was allowed to even touch, let alone tamper. Of course, that could be due to the burgundy satin bustier strapped about her without a centimeter to spare, or the effect of such a large bosom atop the tiniest waist he'd ever seen.

Double whoa.

Jackpot! Gorgeous. Womanly. Spectacular.

The impression didn't fade as he took in the wrist-length black lace gloves with the ruffled edges, the dark mark of a tattoo just above one glove edge, a jagged-edged dark-violet mini-skirt fashioned in some brocade-type fabric. And then he factored in her legs. Stunning. The chick was stunning. Legs like that didn't need the added enhancement of thigh-high black crocheted stockings, nor the ankle-high button-edged boots. That was just overkill. All-in-all, it was hard to tell which part made her the most beautiful thing in this part of the world. It was hard to decide. Hell. It was even hard to breathe. She might as well have shoved the point of her umbrella through him. Jake gulped and stuffed the reaction down.

"Who…are you?" His voice was ragged. Choked. *Shit.*

"A complication you're about to deal with."

"Oh. I'm game, Baby. Complicate away."

The motion with her umbrella stopped. Her eyes narrowed though the blue stood out even then, still striking.

"Oh. Bother. I'd heard you were a player. I forgot the word has more than one connotation."

She had a killer British accent. Everyone on security detail tonight was getting a bonus. Hell. Double bonus. "Who'd tell you such a thing?" he asked.

"Your dossier."

He had a dossier. As if this was a movie set for an espionage film. Jake grinned and launched onto his butt on the edge of the pool. Settled. Silently gave kudos again for having the foresight to put in-floor heating in all his rooms. Even here. And then he looked back up and over at her.

"If my dossier says I'm anything less than completely yours, Babe, then it's an out-right lie."

The umbrella rose from the water, putting little drips onto the surface. She didn't appear to notice.

"I suppose you think you're being charming," she told him.

"No suppose about it, hon. I *am* charming. And you're gorgeous. You got a name?"

"Cassandra."

Man. What a perfect name. Said in an ear-pleasing voice as hot as any Southern hemisphere beach sand. With that accent. It was going to haunt him. She'd tipped her chin to sound out her name, putting emphasis on all three syllables, just in case he couldn't get it. That was pulse-stirring. Or maybe that came from the perfect enunciation she gave it. Her accent really was to die for.

"Cassie? Hmm. Great name. Totally fits."

"Cassandra."

She corrected him. He ignored it. After all, it was his house.

"You know, Cassie…I'm going out on a limb here but I rather like puzzles, and you're definitely presenting one. You're from England. Am I right?"

"Maybe."

"No maybe about it, Babe. I've got a great ear for voices and accents. You're definitely British. That accent is a dead giveaway."

"I could be Australian."

"No way. You speak the words with perfect accuracy. Aussies like to slur. I'll take my guess a little deeper. I'm going to say…London. Born and bred. I'd say James Street, but it's hidden behind an East end accent you've worked hard at. How am I doing?"

Her eyes weren't narrowed anymore. He wouldn't put it quite at wide-eyed, but her gaze had way too much impact through that little lace veil. He should probably find a towel. Or a robe. Or get back in the pool. Or…just pass all the bullshit jargon, and get naked.

With her.

That thought lifted more than goose-bumps. Pleasantly. Rapidly. He hiked a knee to keep it to himself for the moment.

"I've been known to frequent the area."

She finally answered him as if he'd been wrong. Jake lifted one side of his mouth in the half-smile he was noted for. Most girls said it was his best feature. That was before they saw the entire package, of course.

"Right."

Her frame lifted in a little sigh. "Oh, very well. I frequent the streets. The clubs. Sometimes the alleyways. The Underground. It's good hunting ground."

Wow. Did that mean what it sounded like? And just how did he get this lucky?

"Hunting." He didn't ask it. It wasn't a question.

"Oh yes…hunting."

Grant me stamina. Please.

"Just keep talking, Cassie. Anything. Say anything. Anything at all."

"Why?"

"That accent. The view." He whistled lightly. "I have to tell you Sweetheart, your hunt is over. For tonight anyway. And I mean over."

"You really are cocky."

She didn't know the half of it. Jake snickered. "Your dossier missed that part? I suppose it missed the hefty bank account and genius IQ, too."

"Oh no. Of specific note is a massive ego and just as massive bank account. There was a highlighted section about your intellect. And there was even a bit in there about your affectation to swimming timed laps. In heated pools."

"I was a state champion swimmer, Love. Good thing. I'm lazy, otherwise. In case you missed it, swimming's great for creating six-pack abs and then keeping them ripped. You ladies seem to appreciate that, and since I appreciate you ladies, it's a double win."

"Do you say anything that isn't a come-hither?"

He ignored her jibe. He'd taken on tougher chicks than this one. It was a challenge and he loved those. It made their cries of pleasure when they melted even sweeter. He cleared his throat. "Swimming doesn't do a thing for upper body size, though. I have to spend time working weights for that."

"Hmm. The file did say a bit about a weight room. Track. Sauna. Spa. Jacuzzi. A fully-equipped regulation gymnasium."

"You want to see it?"

"I'd rather see your gaming chamber."

"Whoa. And here I thought you didn't like come-hither remarks."

"You really can be rather annoying."

"I'd rather peg it persistent."

She pursed her lips. As if expecting a kiss. And that just kicked his heart rate a bit faster. She had perfect lips, too. Kissable. That was basically all he could see of her face. It was enough. It didn't matter what the rest of her looked like. That was odd, but in a good way. He was getting a bit of mystery with the snappy put-downs she kept spouting; each one demanding retribution. They were delivered with perfect precision with that throaty, warm, accented voice. He was enjoying every moment of this. It was intriguing. Absorbing. Captivating. Maybe too many other women were just too blatantly available, taking all the fun out of it.

"I refer to your game playing chamber," she informed him.

"Me too. I've got an extra-outsized king bed, too. Special ordered. Perfect for playing the oldest and best game in the world, Love."

"If I called you annoying, I was mistaken. Obnoxious is more appropriate."

"Thank you. I do try."

"You're trying to be obnoxious?"

"Not really…but if it works, I'm all for it."

"Works at what?"

"Interesting you."

That stopped her for a moment. Her chin actually lifted, giving him a slight glance at perfect cheeks, and a flash from those blue eyes. And then she tipped her head fully back and laughed. Sweetly. Unashamedly. Perfectly. Dragging his mouth into an answering grin. Damn! There wasn't anything about her that didn't pull at him. She was absolute perfection. She brought her head back down and sniffed slightly as if she'd laughed so hard it brought tears.

She must not laugh often, or hadn't expected it, because her mouth altered. She wasn't smiling. Her lips were in a thin line as if deep in thought. That sort of look wasn't remotely in the cards for tonight. And he just had to change it. So he started talking since she just stood there, silently regarding him, as if any levity was his fault.

"Does that mean…it's not working?" he asked.

"My interest in you is a given, Jacob. I mean…look about. I'm still here, aren't I?"

She gestured with the umbrella to the room at large before putting the tip into a tile joint for stability. Then she added to that stance by clasping the handle with both lace-covered hands in front of her. At her waist. That pose looked a lot like a poster for a French Revue. It gave him another shot of pure male awareness where the sharkskin briefs were too tight. It also gave him some measure of her height. Or lack of height.

"You can call me Jake," he offered.

"Maybe later, Jacob. After we've discussed our business."

"We have business? You're joking. Tell me it's a sham and this is some sort of set-up the guys arranged. Please?"

"I have business to conduct, Jacob. That's why I'm here. I'm not so sure about you."

"Truly? I've lost my touch."

He heard a sigh.

"You're very entertaining, Jacob. Truly. But I've got business to finalize. Before seeking anything like pleasure."

Holy crap. His spine even felt the fiery sensation from that last word. It made his response tremble before he caught it. "Well…get on with it, then."

"You enjoy gaming?"

He sucked in his cheeks while he regarded her. "Didn't we already cover this? My game playing chamber is presently off-limits…unless you mix business and pleasure. And I have to tell you. I'm on if you are."

He got a slight shadow of a smile for that quip.

"Let's keep it simple, shall we? Brief. And if we cease the double-entendres, the pleasure portion will come all the sooner."

"All right. Shoot. What do you want to know?"

"When I spoke earlier of gaming, I meant the video gaming craze, and your immersion in it. Your dossier is full of references I didn't care enough to read, nor wish to take the time to understand."

"Sounds like great reading. I have got to see this file. But it's more than a craze, Sweetheart. It's the closest thing to adrenalin-kicking reality this side of warfare. You insult with few words. Craze, my ass. Video gaming is the future, and I'm neck deep in it. I create and market video games. It's a dream job and grants me a dream life. It's what I do for a living, and as you already noted, I make a great living. The ladies seem to like that part, too."

"Tell me about it."

"What the ladies like? Or how much they like it?"

"That is not what I asked. Nor is it brief, although it is simple."

"I'm working with you on this, Sweet. Trust me. You've got the carrot firmly attached to the stick, and this fellow is totally focused on it. What part of the video gaming industry do you want to know about?"

"The games. I'm especially interested in the one named *Bellus*. Or, to be more specific, the part of the game that you named *Daemon Bellus*."

Act stupid, Jake. He knew her game now. But she was the best damn spy his competitors had ever used. "*Bellus*, huh? Not sure I recollect that one exactly."

"Must you lie? Now?"

"I've got a lot of projects, Love. My calendar is full of them. A lot of ongoing ones, as well as a few upgrades. Describe it."

"*Bellus* is the best-selling game in the country, making you millions by the hour…and you expect me to believe you can't recollect it?"

"I don't track money. I have accountants for that. I made my first million while still in high school with my VIDWAR game. Why do you think I left MIT? Couldn't make the grades?"

"I didn't ask. I don't care. And you're not helping. I need to know about the thing called *Daemon Bellus*. There's a character called Dane in it. You recollect it? Dane is a vampire player – who morphs into a Viking – and then becomes a berserker. I'm very interested in that particular aspect."

"It's called an avatar, not a character. And *Daemon Bellus* isn't a thing, it's a mode."

"So…you do recollect it?"

Shit.

"And now you'll tell me about it, and our business will be conducted, and we can move on to other things. Yes?"

"Look, Cassandra." He stressed all three syllables on her name. It just felt right. It was impossible to tell a layman about designing a video game. You either spoke the lingo, or you didn't.

"Yes?"

"I can describe the programming. I can tell you about the scene-setting, mode enhancement, and assigning limits. I can't tell you about the marketing and packaging and distribution. That's what I have strategist and marketers and shipping consultants and analysts for. Nor can I describe the actual play. I don't spend time on them once they're on the market. If I did that, I wouldn't be envisioning my next one. I've got one hell of an idea right at the moment. Want to hear it?"

She'd moved somehow, bridging the distance between them in a skim of motion, snatching his spa robe with the umbrella tip as she went. And she'd done it without one hint of stride, and little time. Jake blinked against the impossibility of her approach, even as he got a perfect view up her legs. Damn. If he wasn't mistaken, she wore a pair of old-fashioned bloomers, complete with a little black bow right at her…

"Get dressed. Show me." She dropped the spa robe into his lap.

Jake sighed heavily and grabbed the garment before springing to a squat, gaining his feet beneath him. From there he slowly rose to his six-foot, three inches. Two hundred two lbs. Perfectly sculpted. Toned. Fit. He didn't have to flex, but something perverse just made it happen. She was just as dainty and petite as he'd suspected. That little black hat would fit beneath his chin. If she were closer. He watched the cobalt blue of her eyes disappear for a few moments before it was back. As if she'd closed them for a lengthy blink. And then she licked her lips. He didn't have to guess that. He watched it. He only hoped the slight jerk of his frame wasn't as visual as it felt.

CHAPTER THREE

Jake led the way. It wasn't a far walk from the pool room to his private domain. He'd named it Walsh Command Central. And then he'd trademarked the name just for grins. The place was one gigantic space, with differing floor levels accessed on any side, black matte, sound-proof walls, chrome fixtures, and lighting that could be dimmed by voice control. The area was usually jumping with activity since he'd filled the space with a plethora of the largest flat-screen televisions he could order, hanging like wall dividers, all mounted at optimum viewing level; the bottom frames starting just at knee level for a couch potato gaming junkie. He knew. He had configurations of couches and chairs strategically placed on every level for that reason. They were great for making sure he had the right effect for his creations.

The room contained four 1200 watt, 7-speaker sound systems, installed in the walls, every gaming system available - in the latest versions, and...heck, he'd even designed a special room for all of his archaic computers, including the ones from boyhood. That area held every facet of his career –

every idea he'd come up with, the story boards, the design efforts that ensued...everything – the successes as well as the failures.

Walsh Command Central also had an alcove on the top level, set up as a mini apartment for the times he lived there, filled with inspiration and adrenaline. The bed wasn't super king-sized, but he didn't think they'd need the space. Then again, every single one of his couches could be put to use, if need be.

He jogged up two half-flights of steps, disdaining the polished chrome rails running along the walls. He didn't need handrails. Yet. And if he got too damn old and decrepit to use the stairs, he had two elevators. Those rails were installed for visual effect since they reflected the tiled floor and elongated the space. They were necessary for home insurance reasons, too, in the event anyone slipped. He got the instantaneous notion that they'd work perfect with handcuffs. He envisioned several bondage scenes he was going to incorporate into his next video game. Featuring her. Or an avatar very like her.

He knew she followed behind him. He didn't check. He *felt* her. She didn't speak. He returned the favor. For the moment. Silence was its own reward. It was also a tad odd now that he thought of it. He couldn't even hear her steps. His wouldn't make much noise, he was barefoot...but those little ankle boots of hers had heels. They should be making some sound. Jake cocked his head slightly to listen as they neared the double doors crafted of smoked glass, etched with WALSH COMMAND CENTRAL in huge letters that sparkled in the right lighting. *Nope.* Couldn't hear her. Not a whisper of sound betrayed her presence. He sure hoped the cameras were getting this.

He swiveled and she almost ran into him. Almost. He watched her jerk to a stop just before her nose hit him right between his pecs. Her proximity raised goose flesh all along his skin…and something else. Something he'd never felt before. Like an elevation of every cell in his body. As if there was an electric zone between them. It was a weird sensation. Truly weird.

"You've some reason for stopping?" she asked his chest.

"Before we enter my domain – my *private* domain – we need to get some clarification."

"Why?"

She was still talking to his chest. That was okay with him. He was actually having trouble breathing. Every inhalation contained some aromatic essence that added emphasis to the elevated awareness happening to him. If she actually looked up at him, she'd probably see it, and she had enough put-downs for him already without adding what had to be lust to it. Or, was this lust? He couldn't remember feeling anything like it. But it had to be lust, or something just as primitive. Feral. Strange. Wholly remarkable.

He cleared his throat. "So I can decide how to proceed."

"Proceed?"

"Are you looking for something specific…or are you on a fishing expedition?"

"Why?"

She asked it to his chest again. He lifted it with the force of his inhaled breath before letting it out slowly. That was stupid. Every ion seemed filled with her particular fragrance, and he'd just gotten a lungful of it. He could swear bells were ringing in each ear. And that was just more weirdness. He'd come up against female sirens before; partied with women blessed with sensual allure; been matched against women sending sexual stimulus with every breath.

This Cassandra had them all beat.

"Because I can take you directly to what you want...or I can wade through a lot of fishing line while I try to figure it out. And that carrot is powerfully tempting, Cassie."

"Cassandra."

She corrected him, using three, perfectly enunciated syllables. Again. It was sent with just enough emphasis at his chest that his heart stuttered. More weirdness. He should probably have closed the robe before tying the belt, but she'd acted like his physique wasn't worth a second glance and that had smarted. That just made something perverse in him want to show off a little more skin. And that just got him more of this odd sensation from her proximity to his bareness.

"Don't you think that's a tad formal, Love? I mean...let's recap, shall we? We've got a quick stop in here and then we're heading right to pleasure central. Let me emphasize that: *Pleasure* central. And really. It'll be hard to slide my tongue along your skin if I have to do it while saying that mouthful, Cas...san...dra."

Her chin came up and those cobalt eyes seared right into him through the lace veil. Or felt like they did.

"Who said anything about your pleasure?"

Jake lifted a hand and pulled at his earlobe as nonchalantly as he could while he considered her. And then he puckered his lips with the reply. "Oooh. Ouch. You know, Cassie, you're not the only female on the planet. I can have any woman I want. Any. All I have to do is call. And not even very loudly."

"I'm not just any woman, Jacob."

He snickered. "I'll bite."

Her lips curved into the sweetest smile he'd ever seen. Or could remember. He pondered them as he considered going in for a kiss, and then stifled the urge. *Not yet, Jake my man. Not yet…*

"And you can't have me. No one can."

"Whoa. Do I ever love a challenge. How did you know?"

She tipped her head back and trilled the laugh again. A lengthy one, her mouth open and showing off pearly white teeth and what looked like…fangs. Real, honest-to-goodness fangs. They looked rather sharp, too. Jake instantly responded, the reaction moving him back a full step. That was so disconcerting, he almost grabbed for one of the hall rails beside the doors in defense.

Her head came back down, her mouth closed again to any feature he must have imagined, and then she licked her bottom lip. His entire frame pulsed at that one little thing. The slight glimpse of a tongue. Sliding onto those ruby-red lips.

"You're very amusing, Jacob. Very."

"Is that a mark in my favor?" The words sounded raspy, probably because they came through a dry throat. He swallowed to fix it, but it was more a gulp.

"Oh. It's one of several. I assure you."

Wow. Double wow. His skin started to react at her answer, sending an itching sensation all along every limb. Almost like it was craving her and pissed off at the denial, too.

"Now, can we get back to our business?"

"And I already asked. What...do you want? Specifically?"

"How did you know about Dane?"

He'd almost turned around to press his thumb against the ID fingerprint panel built into the handle that allowed entrance to just three people: Him, and his closest frat buds, Daniel and Sam. Those same guys were supposed to control access to him since they alternated weeks as heads of his security. Tonight was a farce. The red-head looking at his chest was proof. They were all still getting bonuses.

"Dane?" he repeated.

"Yes...Dane. You forget already? I'm here to find out about *Daemon Bellus.* Especially Dane. He's the Viking vampire character from your game, the one who goes into a berserker phase and rips through opponents. Him."

Jake blew a sigh hard enough it lifted his hair from where it had dried on his forehead. "My Viking is named Dane because it sounded sexy. if you can believe that. I originally wanted Eric, but my marketing gurus vetoed it. And let's get some of the jargon straight. Dane is not a character. None of them are. They're avatars. Berserker is a gaming mode not a phase. And I got news for you, Cassie. I made him up."

She looked confused. At least, her mouth did. And she didn't even balk at the use of his nickname for her. *Sweet.* He just might be getting to her. And then she shook her head as if reading his mind and negating it.

"No. I don't believe it. It's too perfect. Too close."

"To what?" he asked.

"What of the Slavic character — I mean avatar?"

"Which one? The Hun?"

"The lady."

"Oh. That would be Natalya. What about her?"

"She rips through people's chests to grab their hearts out. How did you know that?"

"Pretty cool stuff, huh? I made that up too. She's an invention. They all are. The ninja chick, the Hun, the inside trader guy in the navy pin-striped suit…even my Canadian Mountie. They're all from in here." He tapped his forehead.

She looked unconvinced. At least her mouth did. And he was getting tired of basing everything on that little bit of her face.

"Is that what your little visit is all about? Copyright issues? Because if I've tromped on somebody's trademark, you'll have to call the legal office during business hours. My lawyers check and triple-check everything. There's not one reference to anyone or anything real, dead, or already fictionalized."

"You made them up? Truly?"

"You're joking, right? Or…are you one of those insane gamers? The kind that gets so fixated on a game, they actually start thinking its real? 'Cause it's not. It's a game. It's fake. Nobody gets killed. Nobody turns into an immortal creature. Only crazy people think it's real."

"Don't offend me."

"Look who's offending. Let's get this straight right here and right now, Babe. Nothing in my games is real. Nothing. Ever. I even design the settings. Castles. Swamps. Cemeteries. Wastelands. All of them. And the avatars? Not real either. Sorry. The Viking isn't real. He's a vampire, and everyone knows they're not real. Neither are gargoyles. Werewolves. Demons. Trolls. Angels. Fairies. Dragons. Aliens…hell. None of it. And let's just face facts. Berserkers are a thing of the past, too, if they even existed then."

"I said, don't offend—"

She poked her index finger into his chest and the entire world went off-kilter. The hallway rocked. Swayed. Lightning-type fire slammed through him and then it rocketed right back out, leaving him standing rooted to the tiles, breathless and shocked, and tingling all over with excitement. And that was just from one fingertip?

CHAPTER FOUR

"Whoa. Babe. Did you just feel that?" he asked.

"Hush," she replied.

"That had to be an earthquake. In New Hampshire? That'll hit the news. I'm talking major quake here. Close to seven in magnitude."

"I said…hush."

She ended her words with a "shhh" hiss. And he actually obeyed. It had something to do with how he was still sucking for breath, but probably more with how she lifted her hands into the space between them and worked at the four little buttons at the right wrist of her lace glove. He watched it with complete absorption and absolute anticipation.

Wow. That was even weirder. He was salivating and panting, while other parts elongated and hardened until the confine of sharkskin trunks pressed back in reply. And for what? A glimpse of the hand beneath a glove? What the hell? Jake was used to women dropping everything in his presence – including their underwear. Harems of women. He'd seen everything and experienced more. And yet this Cassandra chick had him glued to the sight of little pearl buttons leaving their loops. He didn't even dare blink.

She pulled her fingers out, one at a time, and held the glove in her left hand while rubbing her naked thumb pad all along her fingertips. Jake licked his lips. Stumbled through a shaky breath. Groaned inwardly. Her hand was finely boned, the fingers long and slender, and she had soft-looking, really white skin. She wasn't the type to frequent nail salons, either...not for the fake nails anyway. Her nails curved along the tops of each finger, and there wasn't a speck of polish on any of them.

She was absolute perfection.

She'd finished testing the sensation on each finger, and then she looked at her palm before turning it outward. Toward him. And then reaching for him. In slow motion. And the closer she got, the more his body tensed. His rod strained against the trunks. Hard. Needy. Every portion of his body felt as if it did the same. Readied. Primed. Anticipating. Her palm neared his abdomen. Every muscle he owned coiled. And then she touched him, pressing lightly against his six-pack, and reality took a hike.

Again.

This time he got sound along with the riot of other sensations. The hallway about him rocked. Swayed. Rotated. Jerked. All accompanied by a musical symphony of bass notes that throbbed through each ear, taking their rhythm from the waves of heat radiating from where her hand rested. Against him. Jolts of electrically charged sensation emanated from where she touched, pulsing through every limb, sending something so close to ecstasy in their wake he gloried in it. And then he shook with it. And then he pulled up to arch backwards, smacking his head into the glass doors behind him in order to emit a solid groan of sound that blended nicely with the tones resonating through each ear.

She lifted her hand away, stopping every sensation in that exact instant. The echo of his cry faded. Jake opened his eyes and took in the LED fixtures all along the ceiling of his halls, bravely sending light from their antique-styled fixtures even as they blurred. He was close to sobbing at the absolute cold and bereft feeling overtaking him, consuming the warmth and pleasure she'd just given. He blinked rapidly against the instant emotion and had it conquered before he brought his head back down to look at the top of her head. And that ridiculous hat. He probably snarled. It was the best he could manage.

"What…just happened?" The first word was a croak. The rest wasn't much better.

"Oh, Jacob."

Damn it! Her voice carried a hint of tears. It just made his eyes water up again. That was the absolute last thing that could happen. Jake blinked with machine rapidity, and when that didn't work, he moved his vision, looking over her head at the opposite wall. His muscles were slowly relaxing, although they still burned with use, as if he'd hefted an economy sized car, and somehow survived holding the weight. He focused on his breathing, filling his chest with air, holding it, and then exhaling it. Slowly. Efficiently. Just as he'd learned in Tai Chi. Long breath in. Hold. Count to eight. Release it slowly. Count to eight. Inhale. Hold for eight. Exhale. He kept his mind on counting and breathing and finally managed to conquer the urge to cry.

She was fussing with something. He heard the whisper of material. Or something. He moved his glance back to her. She'd removed her other glove. They rested on the floor beside her boots. Those gloves looked expensive. Real lace. Hand tatted. Old. Strange that she'd just drop them. She had a little ring at her middle finger, at its center a really high grade ruby. That probably cost a pretty penny, too. Everything about her smacked of value and old money. And tons of class.

She lifted her veil over the hat. He watched it come across the mass of red-wine-shaded hair that comprised her bun. And then she moved her head, grazing his frame with her gaze as it traveled up his chest…reached his neck. His chin. And then her eyelashes fluttered a moment before she brought her gaze right to his.

Pow!

The feeling was equivalent to a blow. Right between the pecs. It stopped his heart before that muscle decided it might as well keep thumping away in there. Jake didn't move anything as eyes bluer than any he'd ever seen looked right into his. Deeply. Absorbingly. Questioningly. Closely enough he saw every slight variation of blue about her pupils. He couldn't see a lens ridge, but that didn't mean she wasn't wearing them. That eye color just couldn't be real. He added to that. *She* couldn't be real. This couldn't be real. Nothing like her existed. It couldn't. He was asleep, and he was dreaming. That was it. Women this inherently beautiful just did not exist. Jake fancied himself an expert. He'd seen it time and again. Take away a woman's make-up and you took away a good percentage of her comeliness.

Except this one.

Cassandra didn't appear to use anything from a cosmetics counter. Everything about her looked the purest of natural. The most pristine. And he'd denigrated her. She wasn't just gorgeous. She was the best looking thing imaginable. Without one bit of artifice. There wasn't a hint of foundation, a flake of eye shadow, a film of mascara. No blush. Lipstick. Nothing artificial got anywhere near that face. The sound hitting his ears this time was a very pleasant high-pitched note. Perfectly played. Like something from a violin master on a Stradivarius. Complete with a vibrato toward the end of it.

"Jacob?" He thought she asked it.

"Yeah?" He might have answered.

"I think…you're my mate."

Urch!

Jake's eyes went wide and he lifted his head away, losing the other-worldly aspects of this near embrace, but gaining a bit of sanity back at the same time. He had to do something. Say something. Anything. Did she just say…mate? *No way.* He had to get this back to his normal affair – a sex romp with a beautiful girl that fitted nicely into a long string of them. That way it could end without ramifications and recriminations. On either side. *Adios, Seniorita. Gracias.* Just like always.

"Did you hear me?"

"Uh…Cassie—"

"You wish to feel it again?"

His knees sagged. He had to lock them to remain upright. She'd probably seen the sway before he controlled it. He let it go. She was handing out weakness with the total male desire rippling across the surface of his skin, making the spandex suit even more restrictive. It didn't disguise much. He was hard and large enough to lift the robe's surface. It wasn't possible to hide any of it.

"Look. Cassie—"

He tried again. She interrupted him again.

"It's not something you can fight, Jacob."

Oh yeah? Well, this guy was swinging and kicking and screaming. He wasn't going down without a fight. Her voice was seduction itself; her scent, more so. The view would be enough to send him to his knees. It felt like he was already fighting every cell in his body, and that just to stay away from her gaze.

"Am I going too fast?"

Oh, hell no. She did not just ask that. No woman had ever said that to him. Ever. A few moments ago he'd have said it wasn't moving fast enough. That was before her touch and the resultant altering of nature. And if that happened from just a touch, what would a caress feel like? A skim of his fingers down her curves? A taste of her lips? He groaned slightly at the thoughts as everything on him immediately craved all that. And more.

"Jacob. Look at me."

He gulped, swallowing audibly. Moved his head back down. Oh, no. She was still watching him, those unbelievable eyes sucking at his gaze. She'd moved closer, too. And she'd unfastened her bun, releasing her hair. He'd been a bit off on the length.

Dark red locks skimmed the backs of her knees. And it was thick even at the ends. Wavy. Shiny. Feminine. That bosom of hers was getting to him, too. She'd also felt something, and her emotion had pushed bountiful breasts he'd noted earlier upward, where they were framed and lifted by black lace. As if for him. A roar of something resembling a flash fire flared into being within him. He began vibrating to it. It was an incredible sensation. And he wanted more. Tons more.

And that's when he lost the fight. Sort of. If pretending to be her mate was the way to get more of her magic – then so be it. He pulled in a breath that trembled.

"This mate thing…uh. It's not—uh. It's not forever. Right?"

She smiled slightly. His entire form jerked. He barely kept from grabbing her up and against him by a sheer act of will.

"I mean, it's just for…the moment. For now. Yes?"

"It bothers you that much?"

Jake opened his mouth and started talking. "It's ownership. Slavery. I mean, my parents told me once they were soul mates. Right. No such thing. They never wed. They just mated. Unfaithfully. And then they grew to hate each other. Until dad passed on anyway. Is that what you mean with this 'mate' thing? I mean, I've firsthand information. It's complete and total crap. Your heart in exchange for a knife to stick in it. Worse than a living death…it's—it's mortal purgatory. Every man knows a woman can't be—"

She stopped him with a complete cheat. She'd jumped up slightly, wrapped her arms about his neck, and pulled his head down so she could plant her lips firmly against his. And fireworks erupted. They shot through his skull, and then the hall, and probably out into the New Hampshire night. She had her perfect fingers threaded through the length of hair at the back of his neck, that bounteous bosom firmly entrenched against his pecs, while creating absolute heaven with her mouth, and then her moans. He felt a spike of pain, as if she'd slit open a cut inside his lower lip, and that was followed by a feeling of such immensity, his entire body trembled. Vibrated. Shook.

She came closer, and he helped. He lifted her against him, supporting her with a scooped arm while she wrapped her legs about his hips, linking her little ankle boots at his lower back. And all of that in order to slide parts of her still undiscovered and hidden against where the sharkskin trunks were in the way. Jake slid his free hand to the waistband of the damn things and then peeled them off, shimmying the garment down his legs, dancing to force it to his ankles, and then kicking the trunks aside. He had to get in his bed. Screw that. He had to get her on a couch. He had to get buried in her. He had to. He couldn't think beyond that. He almost couldn't breathe, except she seemed to be orchestrating them from where she was affixed to his chest.

Jake reached back with one hand, somehow found the thumb ID pad, and with the instant click of the door, he shoved backwards through the portal. She didn't help. At all. She was riding him, with little kicks from her legs, while doing maneuvers with her mouth against his that threatened to liquefy his limbs more than once. He slammed against the back of a flat-screen television, jostling cables and making the entire thing tremble against its fastening in the ceiling. He didn't care if it fell. Even if it was the brand new 2160 pixel, 480 refresh rate, 120 inch, razor thin, flat screen. All he cared about was finding his way around it. He stumbled at the edge of a platform, lurched somehow up the steps without falling, and she applauded that bit of athleticism by sliding her mouth across his cheek to his neck. He felt a never-ending series of shivers. An elevation of every sense. A whisper of sensation like a burn. A bit of wetness as if she tongued her way into the perfect spot.

And then she latched right onto his throat, somehow sending a perfect cohesion of bliss and excitement all the way through him. That combination completely undid him, weakening his legs and sending them sprawling. Jake spun, taking the brunt of the fall with his back. He bounced lightly on leather. It must be his lucky night. Obviously. He'd reached one of the black leather sofas. Didn't really matter. He'd prepared for the floor. All that mattered was making certain the waves of ecstasy she sent with her sucking motions continued. And her moans. Along with her sinuous, writhing motions against him. He moved his head, shoving his chin against hers, until she granted him the same access to her throat that she had to his. And then he was just below her ear, breathing onto skin before sliding his tongue along it, thoroughly enjoying the little bumps that lifted as he licked his way along her neck.

Oh...baby! He gave her goose bumps. And an even more ecstatic sounding series of moans. And then, for some reason he opened his jaw, scraping teeth along her flesh, skinning the surface and raising more than bumps. And at the first taste, everything went to absolute nirvana. Shangri La. Paradise. And heaven. Rolled somehow into one. Jake shifted, rolling to one side before one more jolt got her beneath him, her legs still tightly wrapped about his hips, her woman spot almost melded to him. At least, as closely as it could through his spa robe and her various layers of clothing.

And that was changing.

Both hands delved beneath her little skirt, searching and then finding the tops of her stockings. From there, it was an easy move to roll them in a sequence of motions resembling the butterfly stroke in swimming. Those crocheted stockings hadn't much elastic in them, if any. They rolled easily right over her knees and to where her ankle boots stopped them. She sucked a bit harder on his throat, sending him into an arc of complete and total delight. Joy. Rapture.

Screw the boots. And the stockings. They could stay right where they were. Didn't matter. He yanked his robe apart before getting his hands back under the skirt. Skimming his fingers the entire way up bare flesh that trembled. She was perfect there, too. He didn't have to look. He could feel the even tone of her muscles. The supple strength and perfection of skin that comprised her thighs. Upper legs. The firm globes of her buttocks. Then the obstruction of her undergarment.

"Oh Jacob! Yes! Yes! Oh….please? Yes!"

She'd finished her attention at his throat, and amid pleas and cries for him to continue, he felt her licking at his skin. He didn't care about that, either. All he cared about now was finding a way through these damn lace bloomers of her. Every garment had a waist band of some sort. Some avenue created for donning them and then taking them back off. It only stood to reason. And he finally found it. There was a tie above her waist, well beneath the corset he probably should have taken off. But to hell with that. They had time for real lovemaking later. He had to get connected to her and he had to do it now. Now! The craving that filled him was raw and primitive and untamed. It wasn't going to get halted by some bit of grosgrain ribbon connecting these bloomers with whatever garment she wore above it. He had no idea Londoners wore so much beneath their clothing, and it was just her tough luck. She was losing these panties. Right now. Jake grabbed the material on either side of her hips and ripped the garment apart, splitting the center seam.

She gasped, and he slammed his lips to hers, toying and sucking, and elevating everything to an even higher level of desire. He was riding a wave filled with rapacious, unstoppable, inconceivable need. His chest shoved against her, pressing those breasts upward with his weight. He didn't have to look. His mind saw it for him. Those perfect, large, white globes…without a hint of saline or silicone…smashed against him…

Oh love. Oh sweetness. Oh heaven. His fingers quested for her haven. Found it. Slithered about. She was wet. Warmed. Ready.

Jacob grabbed for her hips to elevate them, and then he drilled into her tightness, feeling the cavern sucking at him, welcoming him, enwrapping him, and then...*oh shit*. Everything stopped at an obstruction that just couldn't be. Time even stalled. And then he lifted his head to stare down at her.

He'd never seen anything to compare to the goddess beneath him, her hair fanning out onto the leather of the sofa, her bosom barely hidden in her corset, her lips plumped and sweet and yet wet with a dark red film that couldn't possibly be what it looked like. Could it? And then he factored in her eyes, sparking with something like blue fire, spearing him right through the heart.

"You're a virgin?"

The whisper was harsh. Guttural. Rough. Filled with frustration and overwhelming male need. Portraying exactly what his rod felt as it continued to pump in little surges against where it was being denied.

"Not anymore."

She smiled after the answer, showing off sharp-tipped canines. *Fangs?* Jake narrowed his eyes on the sight, and then looked down. And that just got him an eyeful of her breasts, barely leashed by her corset. He was mistaken. He hadn't seen fangs. That was just too much to believe.

"Oh...Baby. I'm so sorry. This is bad. Why didn't you...say something?"

Taking a virgin was bad. Taking one who claimed to be his mate was even worse. And taking one without a shred of protection between them had to be the absolute worst. This sort of thing carried penalties. He wasn't this stupid. Ever.

"Ah!"

His cry carried rage that started at his loins, swiftly churned to his lower back, and just moved outward from there, encompassing everywhere it roamed with the same fiery sensation. His shoulders tensed next, taking some of the angered tautness from inside and putting it on vivid display. He was probably bruising the flesh he still held in both hands, too.

"Please, Jacob! Finish. Take me. Now! Please?"

"You don't...know what...you ask!"

His reply came in panted breaths, through gritted teeth, and was accompanied by the slightest push into her. She stiffened and that just got everything he still controlled more tightly coiled. He should stop. They should at least find a rubber. He had to move away. And yet nothing on his body obeyed. His rod tunneled even deeper. Getting gripped tighter. With more suction. While masses of flesh-wrapped coils slipped and gripped as they tried to embrace him. Milking him. He was going to lose it in a moment.

It was her movement that decided it. She lunged upward, lifting both of them as she reached around and grabbed his buttocks. And that unbelievable move was done so she could yank him down fully into her cavern, ramming him to the hilt, while sending a cry that sounded pain-filled and full of recrimination into the room. But that couldn't be, because she was laughing before the sound died. How was it possible? And that was just as impossible as the fact she was setting the rhythm next, using her hands to control his thrusts, pushing him almost out of her. Ramming back in. Almost out. As if he was some sort of do-it-yourself sex toy she'd decided to try out. And that just wasn't happening. No woman had that much strength, and he really was going to explode if she kept it up. And that was definitely not happening. Not tonight. Not ever. Jacob Walsh had a reputation with the ladies. He never took pleasure. He gave it. His satisfaction was always secondary.

He should have known making love to this woman would alter everything. Cassandra turned him inside out with her movements, drove him wild with her continual cries of satiation, and met him thrust for thrust as he hammered his way to fulfillment. Every muscle tightened to the breaking point, his throat tore itself raw with the force of each tormented gasp of breath, his heart thumped in ever increasing strident beats as he pumped against her. Into her. Worked with her. Pleasured her. And when he couldn't hold it back any longer, he finally exploded.

CHAPTER FIVE

"Shut the fucking blinds!"

"Hey guys! Did you hear that? Our Jake's dropping the f-bomb. On us. His closest and dearest friends. And those blinds are already shut, Bud. And locked." The answer came in a low soothing tone, followed by a snickering sound.

"Then dim the lights!"

"Already did that, too. Good thing we know the override codes." The words were spoken in the same even tone. The same hint of laughter was at the end of it, too.

"Then, do it again!"

"You know…if you use your 'nice Jake voice', the audible activation system would turn the damn things off if that's what you want. You wouldn't need to chew us out over it. Then we could all sit here in the dark while you rage at us."

"That's it! You're fired."

"You're just making him angrier, Sam. Let me give it a try."

"Oh. Right. I forgot. You're a doctor now. Fine. Go ahead, Doctor Malcolm. Try out your new psychology degree on Mister Mensa I.Q. here. See if it gets you anywhere."

A heavy sigh echoed so loudly through the room, Jake nearly howled in pain at the volume of it.

"Now, Jake—"

"Shut up," Jake replied.

"Come on, man. Calm down. We're not here for our health. Daniel was afraid you were dying. Comatose. We can see that for a lie, but if you decided to go on a bender you should've alerted him. Then we'd all still be at our own pursuits this evening rather than babysitting you. Take me, for instance. I was schmoozing lobbyists. Lining pockets. Making sure our side gets heard in the video game violence debate. I mean, really. You think I enjoy wearing a tux?"

"Did I ask?" Jake responded after that diatribe.

"Perhaps you could cease acting like a grizzly bear with a hard-on, then?"

"You ever see a grizzly?" Jake's reply came through his teeth. It was still loud enough to add to the effect of hammers hitting the sides of his head.

"No."

"Then just shut up."

"You know…we haven't seen you this bad since that weekend we flew to Bangkok. Remember that little restaurant with the hand-rolled appetizers— what the hell did they call them?"

Another voice inserted the words and the memory. Sounded like Ryan. Speaking at jet engine decibel level. Or thereabouts. Jake cupped his hands over his ears. Why was everything at odds today? He seemed to have gained light sensitivity and hyper-hearing, and with the increase in vision and sound came a massive headache. And he was cold. Not just shivering with a fever, but freezing. Nothing helped. Not the turtleneck sweater he'd donned atop thick sweatpants or the blanket draped across his shoulders. He was still a mass of sickness. It might have been his lucky night, but it hadn't been followed by the same type of day.

"How can we forget that trip? Talk about gastrointestinal hell. Took me a week to recover. Come to think of it, Jake here looks even worse than he did then. And that was close to death-warmed-over."

That was Grant speaking. Their bodybuilder friend. Six, six. Two eighty. Nose tackle size. The man who acted as bodyguard when Jake needed to look like he had one.

"You need something on your tummy, big guy?" Ryan asked.

"You're fired, too," Jake replied.

"You already fired me. A couple of hours ago. I think we're all fired by now. Malcolm? Ryan? Grant? Yep. All fired. We're just waiting for pink slips. Heck. You even fired Daniel, and he's been your buddy since kindergarten."

Jake groaned again. Daniel spoke up.

"You were looking really bad, man. I mean, bad. I'm surprised I didn't call 911. Maybe we should take you to the emergency room. See what's wrong. I mean, just 'cause you're rich and smart doesn't mean influenza or some super-bug can't take you down."

"Why don't you figure out how to make a decent cup of coffee? That would be helpful!" Jake snarled and spat the mouthful back into the mug. This particular effort tasted like ancient, warmed, flat soda water. Or worse.

"That's the umpteenth one we've brewed since we got here," Ryan replied. "Using every combination of your specialty beans. Freshly ground. Each time. We're taking turns. And you call our efforts piss-water. Why don't you figure out what you want and clue us in?"

"All right. Food. I need real food. You could order some. I'm famished, and you're having the kitchen send up crap." Jake slapped a hand to his eyes to shield them from the light. And then he lurched onto the black leather sofa again. On his belly, so he could stick his face against the surface. He was still on this particular sofa, and it carried a hint of her scent, as well as a heavy dose of reverie. *Hmm*. Perfect lips. Body. Face. Moves. And that hair. She'd had tons of it. It had cascaded off this particular sofa like a red wine-hued waterfall.

"Uh…I'm not asking Anton for another dish. You do it, Sam."

"No way. He threatened to walk out when I asked him for a pizza. And you know how that was received. It's still stuck to the 60 inch flat screen television. How about you, Doctor?"

"Call me Malcolm, you jerk. And I'm responsible for the four-course dinner disaster that got tossed down the garbage disposal not fifteen minutes ago. Ryan?"

Jake slit his eyes open and swiveled his face back to the men lounging about on the other furniture on this particular plateau. The light was still bothersome. And he'd never been light sensitive. In his life. The blinds were closed and latched. It was nearly evening. They'd dimmed the lights so far they were almost out. It was still so bright, his eyes watered up.

"Don't look at me. Anton and I don't see eye-to-eye. I don't speak the language or something."

"He's French, but he speaks perfect English. You haven't tried yet. It's your turn. Show of hands, gentlemen. Who's for sending Ryan?" That was Malcolm again.

Hands shot up. Jake would've rolled his eyes but he sensed it would add more pain to his headache. He knew what he needed. He knew what he wanted. Every cell in his body seemed to crave her. Cassandra. It was like she was in his blood…and yet she'd disappeared. She'd walked out on him. Sometime in the early hours before dawn. Probably the moment she depleted him and finally let him sleep. *How could she leave me?* Was all the mate stuff she'd told him just a means to an end? She took what she wanted from him, and then just dumped him? Jake wondered if this was what women felt once the party was over, and they got dropped off.

He'd never thought of it until now. And felt ashamed. That was sobering. He almost felt worse.

"You want me to approach Anton? You're joking, right? That guy asked me out on a date."

"Right. Every man tries to date you, Ryan. It's your movie-star looks. We think you're a homophobe. Go anyway. It's your turn." Sam answered and then Jake spoke up, stopping them.

"Order a steak. Filet. Sirloin. T-Bone. Doesn't matter."

"Steak. Right." Ryan stood up. Grinned. "You want sides?"

"No."

"Medium well as usual. Yes?"

"No. Rare. And bloody."

Full silence followed his request. Silence. Finally. And oddly, the dearth of noise didn't soothe. It just made everything feel lonelier. More bereft. Almost unbearably so. Jake blinked away the mist in his eyes. This was worse than when his mom had passed. He was *grieving*? Ridiculous. He had to get control of himself. He was acting like a spoiled two-year old on a tantrum. The last thing he could do right now was burst out in tears. He'd never live it down.

"Okay. You want a steak? Done. You want it, uh…warmed? Maybe seared? Or you thinking just straight out of the icebox? Or…as they say in Texas: 'cut the throat, wipe the ass, and serve it on a platter'."

Jake took in the looks of shock and disgust on just about everyone's face. He should feel it, too. He didn't. It's the only thing that sounded remotely appetizing.

"Seared," he finally replied and watched the guys relax. And since he'd never studied body language or any of the soft sciences, he didn't know how he knew that.

"On it."

They all watched Ryan leap down to the next plateau, and the one below that, and then he shoved out the glassed doors of Jake's inner sanctum. Where nobody ever came, unless invited. And yet here they all were. Regarding him.

"You decided to join the living again? Thank goodness. We were about to send for an exorcist or something."

"What the hell for?"

Jake put his hands beneath his shoulders, flexed, and did a series of push-ups. Then he sat up. The sun had gone down. He didn't have to see it, he just knew. And for some reason he felt energized. Awake. Aware. And warmer by the second.

"Well...you did have us chasing imaginary women. As if poring over the video feed from security would make one magically appear. For hours now. Ceaselessly. Slow-mo. Frame-by-frame. On every television in the place. Look. You try. We still can't find her. Ryan couldn't even find her. I think that's why you fired him the first time."

The television monitor filled up with a screen split into four sections, all showing a different angle of his pool. Even in slow motion, it wasn't possible. There was his hand smacking the timing pad. There! If he watched for it, and knew where it was, he could just spot the ripple made from where she'd had her umbrella tip. The water was definitely swirling. But nothing was assisting it. He knew about four minutes in slow-motion time later, his spa robe would miraculously drop into his lap. From right out of thin air. While it looked like he carried on a conversation with nothing.

"She's not imaginary. That robe landing right there...is the proof." Jake stood, waited for the sick feeling he'd been dealing with to hit, and when it didn't, he shrugged the blanket off. Then he stretched fully, working the knots out of his muscles. This was truly odd. He'd felt like a week-old, used and discarded dishrag a few moments ago, and now he felt almost well. And it was getting better by the second.

"Okay. Maybe I misspoke. Let's just call her invisible, then. But that's really stretching the bounds of reality, man. She's invisible, and everything she touches is invisible while she's touching it. Then, the moment she lets it go…poof! Visible again. Want me to fast-forward to the hall scene? That's when it gets really interesting. As if everything in the feeds decided to have fog issues. Look. I'll show you. Maybe you need more light."

"Aren't you fired, Sam?" Jake asked.

"Still waiting for the pink slip. Told you. Oh. And the severance pay. You did promise us a generous package."

"Just let me access my program. I'll show you." Jake moved to a table and pulled one of the sides off. It instantly became an active internet pad. A moment later, he was selecting face shapes to begin. He did his own storyboards. Designed his avatars. Sketched everything. She was going to be the frosting to this cake. And he was really going to love drawing that hair.

"You? You're going to find the invisible woman when Ryan's used every code and trick up his sleeve to locate her? He even tried adding a heat signature when one wasn't in the program to begin with. The guy's a genius and you slur him. Good thing he's gone for your meal. I'd help him hit you. The doctor will even help."

"It's Malcolm, jackass."

"All right—Malcolm. You tell me how he's going to do it, then. We all saw just a bunch of shadow and a hint of electronic fuzz in every single hall shot. There isn't much to be seen because Jake's imaginary woman just happens to be invisible, too. And she casts some weird sort of fog that camouflages everything she touches. Just our luck."

"Oh. There's plenty to be seen. And...stop! Freeze it. There! See? There it is. Two little, black lace gloves just appeared. Like magic. On the tile floor."

Jake looked up at the monitor. Yep. There were two little gloves, although on that screen they were about a foot high. He went back to his drawing.

"Start it up again. And...yes. Wait for it. Wait. Wait. There! There's our Jake's swim trunks getting kicked free 'cause they're no longer needed. You sure that wasn't a cigarette gone crazy making all that smoke? Spontaneous combustion? Something physical? Or maybe she's metaphysical...like a ghost?"

"A ghost?" Grant asked.

"Yeah. Ectoplasm might have this effect on technology. At least, in theory. And we don't have much else here. Doctor?"

"I'm warning you, Sam. One more time with the doctor crap and I'm spilling your secrets on the 'net."

"Just be sure and put 'for a good time, just call' at the end. Or better yet, we could run an online ad. Just warn me first. I'll be swamped with calls."

"A ghost. That would be so rad. Impossible...but rad." Grant mused, completely ignoring the rest of the conversation.

Jake continued working as they bandied words. He ignored them for the most part, chuckling occasionally, and when he finally added the ultra blue shade to the eyes on his drawing, he sent the image to the screen, overriding everything already there.

He should have played a drum-roll for the reaction he got the moment Cassandra's drawn image filled the screen. Exclamations and choked words and more than a few expletives filled the area. It wasn't her exactly, but it was pretty damned close. The mass of red hair. The cobalt blue eyes. The perfect, pristine skin. Lush lashes. That mouth. Bosom. The itty-bitty waist.

"Somebody hit me!" Sam swore. "*That's* your invisible woman?"

"You got to be kidding. No. I don't believe it. No." That was Grant.

"We put an avatar like that in a game, and I'm going to need a lot more funding for the lobbyists just to keep our mature rating," Malcolm joked.

"What's going on?"

Ryan appeared from around the side of the screen, carrying a platter with Jake's steak on it.

"Jake drew his invisible dream girl. To prove a point or something. I guess he didn't think we believed him. Look for yourself. We're incapable of speech at the moment."

"What am I supposed to—? Wow! I mean...super wow! She's electrifying. Paint me neon, somebody. I'm about to light up a sign."

Ryan turned, started speaking, and almost dropped the platter. Jake was in for the save. And then he had his steak supper atop his keyboard pad, and was slicing bites and shoving them in and swallowing. He ignored the cooked portion of his steak. He just wanted the blood. And raw meat. He should be shuddering. Gagging. He wasn't. He was getting an infusion of vitality and strength with every bite. Better than any energy drink. He couldn't shake the sensation. It was odd. Strange. Weird.

"Neon. You're funny. That's probably why he pays you, since you're a crap techno wizard."

"You telling me Jake just drew that?" Ryan asked.

"Why do you think we're all open-mouthed and drooling?" Sam asked.

"*That's* his imaginary woman?"

"You think he's capable of imaging her?"

"She can't be real."

"Well, I want to know why you can't find that vision of woman on the video feed. I thought you were the best. You can find anything anywhere, encrypted or not. But not her? I think you better try again," Sam said.

"And try harder," Grant added.

"She can't possibly be invisible. It's too unfair to contemplate. Are those breasts real?" Ryan asked.

"Careful boys. I'm the jealous type," Jake said, just before shoving in another bite. He was getting warm. Too warm. Making him wonder why he'd donned a turtleneck sweater in the first place. He had passive heat radiating from floors and walls and here he was, wearing a turtleneck. Even knit from Marino wool in the finest gauge imaginable, it was too hot. He yanked it over his head, chucked it across the top of the sofa, and went back to eating.

"You are not."

Jake swallowed and stood, hiked his pants back to just below his waist, and then gestured at the screen behind him. "About her? Guys. Please. Just try me."

"All right. No hitting on Jake's invisible woman. Everyone got that? Now, get me a fresh download of that video feed. Or give me the IP address. I'll work on a board. Move over."

Ryan dropped into a spot beside Daniel, and started shoving a finger along the surface of another mini-screen.

"You get a fresh dose of inspiration, did you?" Malcolm sent the jibe.

Ryan flipped him off with a raised middle finger. Left hand. His right hand was busy moving items on the screen. "If that woman is in this feed, I'm finding her. And maybe…just maybe…if I'm really lucky…she'll have a twin sister."

"Screw that. Find triplets," Sam replied.

The floor trembled beneath Jake then, sending a murmur of it through him. And then a whisper of sound touched his ear. It was his name. Spoken softly. With that killer accent.

"Jacob."

Jake steadied himself by opening his stance, riding out the sway until it ebbed and then ceased. He sent a glance at his companions. Nothing had altered. They were gathered about Ryan. Watching his machinations on the little screen or looking at Jake's rendition of Cassandra. Another tremor scored the floor, making it feel like it buckled. He rode out the motion. This was impossible. That didn't mean it wasn't happening.

"Jacob?"

The whisper got more definitive as if she'd gotten closer. It also carried a worried note, as if he wasn't standing rooted to the spot, every hair on his body rising to alert status. That's when he started wondering if she really was a ghost. Or some other metaphysical manifestation that only the weak-minded experienced. And if she was, he started wondering what the hell he'd do about it.

"Jacob?"

"Waiting, Babe. Right where you left me."

He whispered it, turned slightly, and watched as from the same exact place Ryan came from around the television, Cassandra did. Just like that. Soundlessly. Gliding along the floor toward him, her eyes locked with his as she neared. His heart was like a caged thing, hammering at his chest for escape. His blood was flying through his veins, filling his ears with a high pitched note.

She was wearing a different outfit, but not by much. The corset-thing strapped to her upper torso was fashioned from jade green satin, the jagged-edged mini skirt from several layers of black lace. She wore thigh-high embroidered stockings this time, and another pair of little ankle boots with buttons up the outsides that looked like they'd been carved from real jade. It closely resembling last night's ensemble, only with this one she wore a wide-brim hat, complete with black veil. She was breathtaking. She took every bit of his air.

And then one of his friends finally saw her.

CHAPTER SIX

This assignment was dealing out firsts. Always before, she'd hunt the target down, lift her veil, crook a finger, and once he came near, he was a dead man. Most of them died with a smile on their lips, because draining a man of his life fluid had a pleasurable side if done right. And Cassie liked seeing them experience that. Complete pleasure followed by death. It was payback for what the young viscount had done to her. Yet this Jacob Walsh assignment? Everything about it was a first. She felt renewed. Everywhere. Deliciously so. Fresh. Vibrant. Pure. She knew why.

She'd found her mate.

It was still unbelievable. And she'd been so fixated on getting back to him she hadn't even noticed he had other humans with him. Lots of other humans. That sort of mistake doomed a mission, even an easy one like this one. All she'd had to do was find the person behind a certain video game. Terminate if necessary. Report. The league hadn't known Jacob Walsh was her mate, though. Nobody could have foreseen that.

She scanned the area of the cavernous room where they were sequestered. She had four potential targets to deal with – four. At least they were grouped together. And then she ignored them again. All she noted and felt was Jacob! Her mate. She'd actually found him. Just like that.

The thought brought such happiness, she probably radiated it. Cassandra took in every facet of his chiseled frame as she approached. He wore loosely-fitting workout pants, riding low on his hips, showing off a good section of him. And his near-nakedness. She licked her lower lip. Her mate was certainly masculine. Handsome. Well-formed. Muscled. Hard. Impressive. Everything about him seemed fashioned to draw a glance of interest. He knew it, too. Why else was he forever putting so much of it on display?

"Uh…Jake?"

One of the other men spoke. Cassandra glanced back at the group. The fellow who'd spoken was big, much taller and broader than her mate. He was standing and looking at her with his mouth open. She usually garnered that kind of response. That's why she clung to shadows and hid her face. The stunned expression was mirrored in the three men facing her. There was one fellow sitting on the sofa, his fingers rapidly sliding all about a little drawing pad thing. It resembled the little boards she'd used in learning her letters a century and more ago, but no stylus, chalk, or writing implement was needed. Just fingers.

The world was changing too fast. She should probably keep up.

"I'm out of words, man. Totally. Even if I blink, she's still there."

"By-the-way, you're a crap artist, Walsh. Complete crap. You should give it up. She's much better looking than her picture."

"And just how the hell did she get in? I've got the entire place on lock-down. Anybody hear an alarm? Anyone?"

The guy on the sofa made an exclamation of disgust. "Will you guys shut up? I'm trying to concentrate here! I think I'm onto something. There's a weird sort of electrical pulse thing in the images. It's faint, but I think I can segment and highlight it. I mean, it's weird. Like something out of science fiction weird."

"Ryan."

The over-dressed gentleman in the suit jostled the sitting one in the shoulder without once taking his eyes from her.

"Give me a minute. Guys, I'm serious. I think I can find her. I do. Maybe if I add a color wash—"

"Ryan."

This time it was a young, freckle-faced fellow tapping the busy fellow's shoulder. He shrugged it off.

"Crap. You guys expect the world, and don't even give a guy time to find dirt. There! All I needed was a few seconds and you all have to mess with me. I want you to know I just did the impossible. There isn't anyone else who could've found that. I'm telling you guys…I'm good. I'm better than good. And I'm not blowing smoke when I tell you if this outline is correct, she's even more spectacular than our man Jake portrayed."

"Uh, Ryan. Will you pull your head out of your ass and look up?"

The big fellow shoved on the sitting guy, knocking the pad off his knee and that had the man jerking his head up and that's when he finally saw her. She watched his eyes widen to the same circle shape his mouth was.

"Holy shit." The man finally said.

"That's what we've been trying to say," one of them answered.

Jake stepped to her, his essence reaching out and enwrapping her even before he put an arm about her and pulled her against bare skin. The instant he did, the fantastic sense of awareness rippled through her. Again. Even stronger than last night. It was incredible. Wonderful. His voice seemed to echo through his chest and into her. She had to force herself to listen to what he said.

"If you're finished, Ryan, I'll do intro's. Gentlemen? I'd like you to meet Cassandra…uh. What a jerk I am. What's your last name, Babe?"

"Braun."

"Cassandra Braun. From London…and not my imagination, as you can see for yourself."

"You suck, man. Totally."

"The fellow speaking is Sam. He's head of security when he isn't giving his mouth a workout with wise-cracks. The clueless guy on the sofa is Ryan. He's a techno wizard. The best. Unless you include me, of course. The large guy in the back is Grant. He makes a great bodyguard when needed. That's Daniel at his side. My other security guy. And lastly, the fellow dressed for a wedding is Malcolm. You might note he's the same size and build as me. Stands in for me with the paparazzi, and other undesirable avenues where I don't want to be seen."

"Like fundraising events," the man inserted.

"Money. Looks. Intelligence. And now the hottest chick this side of the Atlantic? You kill me, man. Totally."

"He means both sides of the Atlantic. And everywhere else. He's just a bit slow. Sam? Apologize to the lady."

Cassandra frowned slightly before turning back to Jake, and looking up. He was watching for it. Olive green eyes met hers. He had the slightest copper shade in his eyes…toward the center. She'd noted everything about them last night. They were just as deep and unfathomable as she recalled. He might as well have visible tendrils reaching from him, binding her against his side. She couldn't stop the shivers. She'd found her mate! Her entire sphere seemed filled with Jacob anymore. The others were mere irritants.

"Uh…you want us to take a hike or something, boss?"

"If you need it in words, you really are fired. All of you," Jake replied. And then he winked and looked toward them, releasing her gaze. Cassandra dropped it to his shoulder. His chest. He didn't have much body hair, although he didn't look shaved. Or waxed. There was the slightest line of light brown splicing his torso, and leading down…

Cassie gasped and shut her eyes. She was too new to this.

"You heard him, gentlemen. After you, Grant. Oh no!"

"What now?"

"I just remembered I left a date at that fundraiser. She's going to be sore. Really sore. What time is it?"

"Now, that's funny."

"Midnight. You better run back, Doctor. Before she talks to the tabloids."

"Oh! And secure the door on your way out. No admittance tonight. You got that, guys? I don't want to be disturbed unless the place is on fire. And even that's chancy. It better be a big fire." The words rumbled through the chest she was held to.

"Sure thing, Mensa. Wait! I'll just take the pc pad with me. You guys need to see this. Oh shit. Grant! You lost my program! You are one big clumsy ape. You know that?"

"Come on, Ryan."

Words accompanied their steps. Away. Down a plateau of steps. Through the doors. And then there was silence. And him. Jacob. The one being that brought every dead cell back to life. Energized her existence. Elevated this afterlife to paradise. Gave everything meaning and purpose. And joy. He was moving, turning her toward him with one arm, while the other came around her, encircling. Hugging her against him. Granting her everything she'd lost. And more she'd never known.

But she had to tell him. Wasn't that part of this? Wasn't that what she'd been told? A mate needed to be willing. You couldn't just take a man and make him undead. She couldn't recall the rules. It was so long ago…and it had seemed so far-fetched.

Then.

She felt his fingers beneath her chin, working at the bow she'd fastened. She hadn't pinned the hat on, so if she tipped her chin just slightly, it would drop off, taking the veil with it. He pulled the ribbons free. She tipped her chin. The hat fell somewhere behind her. A moment later she felt him searching for and then pulling the myriad of pearl-tipped hairpins securing her hair off her shoulders. Each time he pulled a pin, the resultant lock fell, caressing her shoulders and upper arms as it went.

"You're here. Oh…Cass. Cass. You came back."

"Cass?"

She moved her glance to his, and the moment their eyes met reason and responsibility went right out the window, fading quicker than the other humans had. She'd seen a grainy old photo of him from years earlier. He'd been handsome in that. It was nothing compared to the reality. Especially when he smiled, highlighting little laugh lines on both sides of his eyes.

"Cassie is such a mouthful," he replied.

"It's Cassandra," she told him with what was supposed to be an authoritative tone, but just sounded whispered and wanton and eager.

"Are all Brits so strict?"

"No. I—wait."

"What for?"

He lifted her, and bent his head, giving her the slightest hint of breath at her lips with his words. The embrace stole her intentions and tossed them aside. She daren't kiss him. Not yet. She had to keep her thoughts lucid, her motives clear. She had to tell him—

His mouth touched hers. He had an arm about her waist and the other hand at the back of her head, securing her…to him. The hold was superfluous. She was glued in place in order to absorb him, giving and then taking every facet of the kiss. It was too perfect. Too wondrous. She wasn't careful, and a canine elongated, then it sliced, and at the first taste, her knees buckled, heaving her against him.

A moan surged through their entwined forms, coming from both throats, the meaning in perfect collusion. She needed him. She needed the real physical pleasure he gave, and the way he gave it. She craved it. Desired it. Had to have it. Her hands flew about his sides, his back, over his shoulders, skimming along every ridge of flesh-covered muscle, while his fingers threaded down her spine, following the line of her clothing. Up. Back down. Lifting the seventy little hooks she'd sewn there and getting nowhere. That gained her a bit of sense. She had to tell him before she lost restraint. Making love to him was too beautiful an experience. Vast. All-encompassing. It robbed her control. Obliterated her limits. She was afraid and trembling with it. She didn't know if she could keep from draining him. And changing him. She didn't know if she could stop.

"You're…shivering," he told her. "Oh Babe. Are you cold?"

"No, I—Jacob…wait! I have to tell you something."

"The only thing you have to tell me is how to get through this damn corset."

"Bustier," she replied.

His huff of breath carried a hint of laughter. "Fine. Bustier. Whatever. Who fashions such a thing? With tons of little hooks up the back…but not one of them work. It's like they're sewn…closed."

"They are."

"What? Who designs such a thing? Sadists?"

Cassandra put her hand atop his and moved his fingers to the hidden zipper at her side, right at her waist. And heard the sound of metal teeth releasing as the material opened. "Me. I designed it."

"Cute. You designed the skirt, too?"

"I design…all my clothing."

Her words stuttered. The jade colored piece fell to the floor, making a thudding sound beyond what material should cause. Her senses were heightened more than ever. That came from the taste of him. The scent. Touch.

"Really? You should have your own label— never mind. I see you do. CB Designs. You own your own business?"

"Yes."

"In London?"

"I live below my shop."

"Don't you mean…above?"

"No. That's part of what I need to tell you."

"Oh…*Baby*. You're beautiful. Exquisite. Everywhere."

He lost his voice more than once, the words shaky-sounding. Then his body joined in. And all because he'd slid his fingers down the sides of her bodice, cupped her breasts, and lifted them free of material. Reverently. As if she might break. And then he moved his hands to her waist and just held her. All of it stabbing right through to where she didn't think she had a heart anymore.

"This mate thing you spoke about last night. I think I know what you mean."

He lifted his gaze and met hers. Cassandra had never seen anything as beautiful as the sheen atop his eyes. She knew her heart was dead. It had been for decades now. There wasn't any way it could feel a swoop of movement. Yet that's what happened. Because of the emotion behind his words and on his face.

"Jacob, you must listen to me. Before it's too late and we go too far."

"I think that happened last night, Love. And I'm willing to do a repeat here. I'd like to best my stroke. My repetitions. And maybe my timing. You on?"

"But—"

"Will you marry me?"

Her mouth was still open to finish telling him, and the rest of the words became a garbled mess. "What?"

"Marry. Me. As in bridal veil. Ceremony. Groom. Supposedly I'm a hell of a catch. I'm on a few lists of top 50 bachelors, anyway. You game?"

"Oh…Jacob."

She was going to cry. Impossible. Incredible. Her? Cassandra Braun? She'd never cried. Even before. Finding her mate had given her back sensations and passions and emotions she'd thought dead and gone forever. She blinked rapidly at his image.

"I mean, I didn't exactly plan this. It's rather spur of the moment…uh. It's crazy. I know. But I can't shake the feeling that if I don't lock you down somehow, you're going to up and disappear on me again in the morning. And I just couldn't take it. Say you'll marry me. Stay with me. Please?"

"Jacob." She choked on his name.

"Am I failing? Crap. I've never done this. And I know it's sudden. It's more than sudden. It's insane. I'm doing it wrong, too. I should be on my knees. Begging. I don't exactly have an engagement ring, either. And the one I'm going to design will take some time to craft. You might have a hard time lifting your hand. You're pretty small. Probably a five. Maybe a five and a half. Yes?"

"Five and a half?"

"Ring size. You're not going to cry, are you? That's good, right? I should've waited. Done this with caviar and champagne. Showered. Shaved. Put on a tux. I have closets full of them. Hell, I should have hired a full orchestra. And I—wait! I know."

He started prying at the little finger of his left hand.

"I've got a signet ring. From when I was a kid. It might fit. Here. Give me your left hand."

"Jacob."

"Please don't say you're turning me down."

"I have something I have to tell you first."

"Do you love me?"

Cassandra's eyes went wide. He stepped away from her, folded his arms, and started pacing, patting his sides as he went. "I know. I'm rather manic, but I swear, I've never felt like this. I mean…I'm head over heels here. I want to keep you at my side day and night. You got it?"

"But—?"

"You do love me? Yes?"

Cassandra smiled. "You're my mate, Jacob. It's not negotiable. It's not changeable. It's not something either of us can fight."

"And that means you love me? Yes?"

"Jacob, you have to listen to me. I'm not like…other women."

"No lie. Who wants them? I want you. Cassandra Braun. I don't want you to leave me at dawn. I want you here. With me. Always. What's it going to take to get a yes out of you, Babe?"

"Oh, Ja…cob."

"You stumbled on my name. That's promising. Is any of this a yes? You do love me? Yes?"

She nodded.

He blew a heavy sigh, cooling her from an arms-length away. "That's one hurdle over. And you'll marry me? Make me the happiest man in the world?"

"It's…not that simple."

"Of course it is. We go file papers. Find a magistrate. Hell. I'll order one in. I've got enough witnesses here already. And I can't wait to show you off to the press."

"Show…me off?"

"On my arm. I've been press shy for years. Not anymore. I think the world needs to see my wife. I might call the news channel. They're always trying to get a story."

"You mean…a photograph?"

"Photo. Digital. News feed. Whatever it takes."

"I can't get photographed, Jacob. That's one of the things—."

"You're publicity shy? Fair enough. That's why I have Malcolm. We'll send him out with a babe on his arm, while we're honeymooning in Tahiti. Or Bora Bora. Or Nassau. What?"

"You go too fast."

"You said yes. I heard it. Yes? You did. Right?"

In reply Cassandra held out her left hand. The ring was too large for every finger save her middle one. And he kissed it after he slid it on.

CHAPTER SEVEN

She was ready early, moving like a shadow. Silently. Stealthily. Cassandra could've stayed a few minutes longer in his arms. The hangar where her plane sat wasn't but twenty minutes away if she moved at slow speed. If she rushed, she'd be there in five. She was still early. She'd wanted the extra time. Needed it. She planned to memorize every facet of him…and what they shared. She hadn't known love felt like this.

She was so lucky! How was it possible? Some of her compatriots waited centuries. Millennia. Akron was a prime example. He'd had years of existence. None of them graced with a mate. And yet, without a hint of notice, Cassandra got hers. It was pure pleasure just to look at him. And not just at his handsomeness. Although that was striking. It was especially noticeable as he slept, the slight touch of recessed lighting casting shadows that emphasized just how handsome. Virile. Masculine.

She didn't touch him. She didn't dare. Shifting from his arms had almost wakened him. He seemed to know she was going to leave – but how could she stay? The sun was going to be up in less than an hour.

She'd just received the ability to feel again, and while it was the most wondrous thing imaginable, it had a dark side. It carried fear. Anxiety. Worry. They just kept increasing. That's why she hadn't told him. She was afraid of his reaction. Terrified of it. Cassandra Braun. Paid assassin. Vampire. One of the undead. Terrified.

She should have said something the moment he asked her to marry him. Definitely before he took the last film of clothing from her body. And well before the second time, when he'd spent so much time worshipping every inch of her body that she'd been squirming in need and torment that only he could ease.

She hadn't said any of it. The sort of passion they shared wielded an intensity that demanded satiation. And then there was the slow, perfect time afterwards. It had been so sweet. So loving. So…amazing. Jacob made certain she knew exactly what intimacy and love meant to him. There was emotion behind every caress. Every hug. Every word.

He'd been talkative. He'd regaled her for hours – sometimes animatedly, sometimes in a husky soft tone, and lastly in a hoarse whisper – about all the places he was going to show her. All the experiences he couldn't wait to share with her. The children he planned on having that he was already naming. He wanted two. One of each. But if she gave him only daughters, he'd be the happiest man alive. Sons would gain the same emotion. All he wanted was her. Each word added to the worry. Her breast grew heavy with fear, thick with anxiety, and then it filled with dread.

She had to leave. Soon. She was wasting time. She knew he wouldn't understand. He'd think she deserted him again. Cassandra wrapped her arms about her to hold in the hollow feeling. She already felt lost. Alone. Empty. But she'd be back. Tonight. She'd tell him tonight. The moment the sun set and she rose—

A huge blast of noise assailed the space, coming in a high pitched screech of sound that hurt her eardrums. Jake jerked up instantly, his eyes shot open, his gaze pinning her in place. Her expression probably mirrored his.

"Cassie!"

A moment later, he moved, shoving her behind him. There were slivers of wood and projectiles flying at her. From everywhere. Jacob couldn't protect her. They were too accurate. A spike of mesh shot out of the cavernous space, swirling open as it flew, drenched with liquid that burned where it touched flesh. It slammed her against the back wall, pinned into immobility, despite how she struggled. Wrenched. Focused. Worked. The more she moved, the worse the netting ate into skin. The hat brim smashed against her face saved it from the acidic effects, but nothing stopped the fire that ate into her bare arms, upper thighs, and bosom. She bit her lip to still the cries, and then got more. Through the lace of her veil and the close weave of net she saw Jacob fall. He landed hard, rolled, and was back on his feet, a thin spike of wood in his shoulder, leeching blood down his arm. Stark naked. And yet still menacing. A moment later and he'd reached her and started yanking at the ropes.

"Ouch! Shit, Baby! What the hell? I can't—! Damn! I need…a knife!"

His fingers were getting burned. He'd had too much of her fluid. Every time he touched the ropes he jerked back in agony. From behind him she watched the apartment alcove fill with hunters. Thirty. No. More. She quit counting. They all carried crossbows. All aimed directly at her. And then a man stepped to the front, pulling night vision goggles down. He was well formed. As fit as her mate. Dark haired. He kept it closely cropped. Looked near forty. Vaguely familiar.

"Stop that, Mister Walsh, or we'll have to tie you."

"Get this off her! Now!"

"That isn't a *her,* Mister Walsh. May I call you Jacob? That's an *it.* And the answer to your demand is no. Reggie. Hank. Crux him."

Two of them approached, carrying a large crucifix that took all their effort to tote. Cassie hissed and narrowed her eyes, and still saw them slam the cross to Jake's bare torso before the burn cancelled her vision. She slammed her eyes shut, but heard Jake's howl of pain even as it covered hers.

"Looks like we're just in time. Sit down, Jacob. Or I'll force it."

Something hit the floor. There was a thud. A cry. A bit of rustling noise. And then silence.

"Why do they always want it the hard way? Please remember, Jacob, you were warned."

"Screw you."

"Very well. You asked for it."

Cassandra slit her eyes open, despite heat that seared both eyes. They'd placed the cross in front of her. On its own stand. It was too close. It radiated heat. Waves of it. And it sucked at her, draining her energy. It took an effort of will and some pain to move her eyes beyond it and find Jacob. They'd strapped him to a chair; his feet yanked beneath the seat with how they'd fastened his ankles to his wrists behind him. He was breathing hard, and still raging at them.

"Who the hell are you?"

"Hunters."

"No shit. I got that part from the weapons and camouflage outfits. What the hell do you want?"

"In time, Jacob. Everything comes to the man who waits, you know."

Jacob strained against his bonds for a few moments while everyone watched. And then he stopped, heaving for breath. "Damn you! Where's my security? If you hurt them, I swear I'll see every one of you persecuted to the fullest extent of the—"

"Calm down. If by security, you mean the three fellows who attempted to stop us, well…let's just say, the big guy is not going to wake up for some time yet. The other two are pretty much in the same position you are. Tied to their chairs. *In situ.* Only they have clothing on. It's probably warmer."

"Are you insane?"

"No. But you're probably going to think I am before we finish."

"No thinking needed, asshole."

"You know, Jacob…can I call you Jake? This is going to be a lot easier if you cooperate and act nice. In a bit it'll be dawn, and everything will be over. This will all be a really strange dream. You'll see."

"What happens at dawn?"

"We'll untie you. And I'll even give you some pants."

"What the hell do you want?"

"Her. Or rather, it."

"Cassandra? Why? If it's money you want—"

"Money? Ah. She didn't tell you her secret. This is rich. Truly."

"Her...secret?"

Cassandra didn't have a live heart but whatever was in her breast plummeted to the pit of her belly, anyway. It was more painful than every one of the wires and the crucifix combined.

"Your security detail was already onto it. They'd have been in here with the information before long. That's how we found her, actually. An IP address doing an internet search. Cassandra Braun. From London. They've been at it all night. Gained tons of information. I really love technology, don't you?"

The leader was walking toward her as he spoke. Jake was straining against his ropes again, turning his skin red. Her eyes burned too much to keep looking. She shut them and hoped the skim of moisture in them would be enough to salve them.

"Ah. There you are. Miss Cassandra Braun. Lovely specimen. Truly...beautiful. I didn't know that. And then somebody uploaded a drawing of you during their search. Hmm. The artist didn't do you justice."

"You touch her, and I'll kill you!"

Jake snarled it. Despite how it pained, Cassandra opened her eyes. Found him. He'd toppled the chair. One of the fellows hit him with something that looked like a mallet. Jake cried out. He took another hit. Then another.

"Stop. Please?" Cassandra asked.

She shouldn't have said anything. The leader's eyes narrowed and then he gave her a wicked-looking smile.

"Oh. This is classic. And so sweet. He's your mate? Is that what this is about?"

"Please?" she continued, a hint of tears coating the word.

"Gentlemen. Stop." He turned his back on her and spoke to his men. "Jake isn't the issue here. We mustn't be uncivilized. Just put him back upright, and toss some Holy Water on him if he misbehaves again. How much time do we have?"

"Twenty-four minutes."

"Good." He turned back to her.

He was about Jake's height. She'd been wrong on his physique. He wasn't near as fit as Jacob. Nor as handsome. He really did look familiar. She couldn't quite decipher why. The Holy Water they'd dipped the net in must be drying. The webbing no longer burned. And if she could just get that cross toppled...

"There's not much information available on you, Miss Braun. That's not unusual, but your file is almost nonexistent. You're very difficult to find. It's still Miss, isn't it? You didn't wed anyone, did you? Yet?"

"No."

"Good. I really hate making widowers. You know how many Cassandra Brauns are in the record books? Tons. Dozens in England alone. There's one particular one...with a birthday of 1841. We found that Cassandra Braun very interesting. Born and raised in a parish orphanage. No parents listed. That's it. There's nothing else. No death record. Nothing. If I had to hazard a guess, I'd have to say 1862, or thereabouts. You don't look a day past twenty-one. How am I doing?"

She didn't answer.

"About all we managed to dredge up on Miss Braun was a deathbed confession. Want to hear it?"

Oh no. No. She started trembling. The webbing hid it.

"According to sources - and if anyone digs deep enough, they'll find it, too – there's a record taken from a certain Viscount Thornby. He passed to his higher rewards in 1911. I forget the date. Doesn't really matter. He gave the most interesting deathbed confession. According to his version of events, back when he was a lad of eighteen, he came home on vacation from Eton to find the sweetest, most beautiful girl in the nursery of his home. She was working as a governess. Had dark, wine-shaded hair, intensely blue eyes. Like I said. She was beautiful. Ring a bell?"

"What the hell is he talking about, Cassie?" Jacob burst out.

"She knows. I can see it in her eyes. When she looks at me. Time, someone?"

"Eighteen minutes."

The man smiled. "According to Viscount Thornby, he accosted this paragon of beauty late one night, after imbibing a few too many drinks with the friends, and in the resultant struggle, Miss Braun fell. Hit her head on the hearth. Expired. Ahem." He turned his back on her and started walking about, getting louder with his story. "The viscount sent for his friends. They panicked. Gathered Miss Braun in the bedding and hauled her down to Highgate. That's a cemetery, Jake. Once there, they found a pine box. Just a plain affair, that box. And then they found some tools and dug a grave. They selected an unused place, not opened yet...near a high fence that shielded their perfidy. Being young men with little in physical pursuits, and suffering from a lot of brandy, they didn't dig the grave very deep. Barely two feet. If that. And then...when they had a spot ready—"

"Stop!"

Cassie was surprised when the word left her throat. He ignored her.

"Don't you think it needs saying? Wasn't that what you screamed about for six nights and five days? Didn't you curse every one of them while you waited to die? Buried alive. In that little pine box? In the dark?"

She would have collapsed if it hadn't been for the restriction of the lines about her. And he just wouldn't stop talking.

"They heard you. Did you know that? That makes it worse somehow, doesn't it? You moaned just as they shoveled on the first bit of dirt. And they finished with it anyway, attempted murder carrying the same punishment as the real thing and all that. Isn't that right, Miss Braun?"

She didn't answer. Jake did.

"On my God."

"God doesn't have much to do with what happened next, Jake. It seems that Miss Braun didn't die. Not then anyway. We don't even know for sure how long she was in there. Could have been moments, really."

It wasn't. It had been five days. She hadn't any way of telling time, but it had been long enough to scrape her way through the top of the box allowing dirt to rain in on her. It was Akron who'd found her. And saved her. And told her.

"All we really know is that when the viscount went back six days later, in the hour before dawn, the ground had been disturbed. And when he dug, he found the grave empty. That's right. Empty. Did you know he came back, Miss Braun?"

She didn't answer.

"You enjoyed haunting him, didn't you? His confession ends with the hope that your spirit can rest now. He says he tried not to go out at night, and never alone. He'd see glimpses of you if he did. You never aged. Never changed. You'd just stare at him and then disappear. And that's when we knew what you were. Time?"

"Fifteen minutes."

She was going to cut this close. Cassandra worked an arm slightly, rippling the mesh. The ropes had dried. It didn't hurt. And her skin was healing.

"What the hell are you saying?" Jacob asked.

"Isn't it obvious? She a vampire."

There was complete silence for about a second. Then Jacob started laughing. He laughed so hard he rocked the chair. Cassandra smiled slightly at how joyous and unrestrained he sounded.

"For a minute there, I thought you were serious, man. Hell. I can tell you that's not true. She's all woman. And this is ridiculous."

"I happen to be completely serious, Mister Walsh. You might want to spare the levity."

"Call me Jake. And cut me loose. I won't fight. Hell. I just want some pants."

The webbing pulled away from the wall slightly, and then she saw the fasteners they'd used. Cassandra slapped her eyes closed as the effect rippled through her. Every spike had a crucifix or other religious icon etched into it. The more she pulled, the more got revealed, and each one sapped at her strength, riddling her with ill effects. Ingenious.

"Not yet."

"Why not?"

"I don't trust you. Or her. But…in about twelve minutes, you'll see for yourself. And then this will all be over. We'll leave. You can go back to making video games. You'll see."

"Oh, really. What am I going to see? A beautiful sunrise over New Hampshire?"

"Miss Braun here is going to turn to dust. And decay. She'll be a dead thing. Exactly like she should have been over a century ago."

"Right."

"You've been humping a corpse, Jacob. You might want to consider that."

A huge thump echoed through the entire structure. The room went absolutely black. Silent. And then a voice boomed out a name, the sound penetrating everywhere. The moment she heard it, Cassandra's shoulders sagged with relief. Akron.

"Chester Beethan. " Akron intoned it, like he was passing sentence.

A spotlight turned on, highlighting the leader.

"Who wants to know?"

The voice chuckled, the sound eerie and vast. "You attacked and tied humans? Chester. Where are your manners?"

"Akron? It's Akron, isn't it?"

"Perhaps."

"Time?" Chester yelled.

"Eleven minutes."

"Didn't your grandfather teach you any better than this? Aren't you supposed to follow some sort of ethical code?"

"You kill for profit and you're talking ethics?"

"You know, I prefer your grandfather. Where is the general, anyway?"

"It's Lord Beethan to you. He's…ill."

"Hope it's not terminal."

"Not yet. He's had a bad reaction to tattoo removal surgery."

Akron's laughter boomed out. "I heard about that incident. Bad form. All around. Apologize to him for me, will you. Cassandra? We'll be leaving now."

"Like hell you will. This here is sanctified wood. And I'm a fantastic shot. At this distance, I can't miss."

The man had yanked his crossbow over his shoulder and aimed it right at her.

"Tsk. Tsk. Chester. You should know better. Invaris? Hit the lights. Slowly. No need for itchy trigger fingers."

Barely there at first, and then so softly it looked like dawn, the room got illuminated. Where there'd been thirty-some-odd hunters, they were interspaced with an uncountable number of black clothed figures. Faceless. Silent. Frightening.

"Allow me to introduce a few of my 4-D Teams, Chester. You're looking at Red, Yellow, Blue, Green, and Black. I wanted to make sure you understand."

"Time?" Chester asked.

"Nine minutes."

The lights went out again. It wasn't quite as dark anymore since the sun was just starting to tint the sky and somewhere there was a window that wasn't covered.

"You want a massacre for your first battle, Chester? Or are you going to give me Cassandra nicely? That's what I came for. That's all I want. Unless Mister Walsh wishes to accompany us. Jacob?"

"You got to be kidding me," Jacob answered.

"You're her mate. She's yours. I don't separate mates, unlike Chester, here. They give badges for it. You have thirty seconds to decide."

"She's a real vampire? Real? You're talking blood-sucking, undead…real?"

"Eternal life, Jacob. Twenty-two seconds. Don't so much as breathe, Chester. I'm watching you. You know I prefer your father. Even if he is hooked on that damn video game at the moment."

"My father is dead. He died in a car wreck when he was nineteen."

"Not…exactly. But close. I think your grandfather might have his own deathbed confession for you, Chester. Fifteen seconds, Mister Walsh. What's it to be?"

"You want me to decide on life or death? In fifteen seconds?"

"Most people don't get that much time. Ten seconds. Answer please?"

"You're inhuman!"

"In a word. We all are. Decision please? We're cutting it close as it is."

There was a garbled sound. And then a choked word from Jacob. Just one. It was followed by a moan she'd give anything to retract. It carried every bit of her anguish. And they all heard it.

"No."

There wasn't a descriptor for the pain. It radiated outward from where her heart should be. Encompassing. Consuming. Overwhelming. She sensed motion. The flurry of material. Swish of air. Arms reached about her, wrenching her free of the wall. Cassandra got lifted, cloaked by fabric that waved with the swiftness of flight, and then she was deposited in the pine box she'd secured in the darkest section of the jet.

And then there was nothing.

CHAPTER EIGHT

The street she'd decided to inhabit tonight was dark. Rain-washed. Crowded. Full of humans. Lots of potential prey. Cassandra toyed with ignoring the cell phone as it vibrated against her palm. Again. Ceaselessly. Annoyingly. It clicked against the signet ring she still wore. She frowned and moved her eyes from contemplation of the portly fellow she was planning to dine with, down to her lace glove. She was wearing a red lace ensemble tonight. Blood red. The color was dyed into the leather inserts defining the slenderness of her waist. The color continued through the weave of her stockings. And to accent this outfit, she'd placed little touches of electric blue. That included her gloves. She'd used buttons of perfectly matched stones in a deep blue topaz. They matched her hat pins, the fasteners on her bustier, and the ones down on her ankle boots. Some said they matched her eyes. But they didn't say it twice.

"Yes?" she answered.

"Hi Babe."

"Don't call me that. Don't ever call me that. *Ever.*" Her voice went low, somehow hiding the pain. It made it sound more threatening, too. Bonus.

"Look Cassie, I was told to call you. You don't have to snap my head off. Oh. I forgot. You're into knives now. Sharp knives. With surgical edges."

"What do you want, Nigel?"

"Not me. The boss. He said to tell you the Hunters evacuated the Walsh complex. This afternoon. Guess they got tired of sitting around and playing video games while they waited. I don't know how. Jerks."

"So?"

"Have you seen the latest Walsh game? Super cool. Features a gorgeous Victorian-era avatar named—"

"I'm a bit busy, Nigel. Can you…cut this short please?"

A hint of trauma stained her voice. Not enough for Nigel to catch it. Cassandra swallowed. Hard. And then she fought the shivers that heralded the grief-ridden, black-edged nightmare. She focused on the fat man she'd selected for her feeding. Smiled. Watched him work at his tie, as if it suddenly choked. Then he smiled back.

"Akron said you should know."

"Goodbye, Nigel."

"Wait!"

She shut the phone, slid it back beneath the suede lining on her palm, and started refastening the buttons, giving every facet of it her complete attention. The entire time, she was blinking rapidly and with consuming patience on every satin loop. All eight of them. And somehow the combination of effort worked, sending the nightmare of ache to the deepest section of her belly. And there it sat. Dormant for now. Yet still it throbbed, as if to a nonexistent heartbeat, echoing off the cavernous emptiness inside.

Not bad, Cassandra.

She was gaining control. Finally. It had taken weeks just to figure out how to do that much. Weeks, when she'd lain silent and alone in that pine box in worse shape than when the viscount and his friends had buried her in it. Much worse.

Let it go, Cassandra. Let it go.

Her non-verbal command worked. All of that was in the past. Over. Done. She'd had to rise. And feed. Or perish. The only way to do it was with a blocking technique. The images. The emotions. The memories. The agony.

Cassandra moved her hand to her veil and lifted it a fraction, giving the portly fellow a peek before letting it drop. The man straightened and sucked in his belly. That was almost amusing. If anything could be that anymore. Her target had a receding hairline, his teeth needed work, and his suit wasn't from a major designer. His fat was the least of his worries. He didn't bear the slightest resemblance to—

She stopped her own thoughts.

"Good eve, Cassandra."

She started slightly at the voice coming from the depth of shadow behind her and to the left.

"Akron?"

"Yes."

"Here?"

"Ah. London. Wonderful city. Especially the nightlife. Look how busy it is. You can't even get a decent spot for a drink. Or a bit of conversation. The potential for feasting is increasing daily. Why wouldn't I be here?"

"You rarely leave your castle."

"Doesn't mean I can't. With the correct incentive. And London seems to have gained that. You should cut him some slack, you know."

"Why? He's fat. Disgusting."

"Not your mark."

"Nigel? Oh, please." She should have brought a parasol. It wasn't necessary in the dark, but it gave her something to fidget with. Flirt with. Lean on.

"Jacob Walsh. Your mate."

"I don't have…a mate." She actually got the statement out without losing her voice, although the middle warbled slightly.

"You know…I'd heard it was better to have loved and lost than never to have loved at all."

Cassandra snorted. "Meaningless literary twaddle. Worth less than the paper it's printed on."

Her voice broke on the last word. Despite everything. There wasn't any comparison to how it felt to be without Jacob. It was better to be ignorant. The loneliness had no margin. The loss became a bottomless pit. The ache that permeated her was endless and ever-increasing. Nobody could quantify how it felt to lose such bliss – because they'd have to know how the ecstasy felt first. Being without it was an impossible weight. One that just kept increasing until limbs and joints couldn't hold it any longer. And then the body crumpled and had to figure out how to block it and go on.

Or not.

"You mean it's not true?"

The view blurred as a tear cursed her, actually flirting with dropping onto her cheek. Cassandra tightened every muscle she controlled and forced the grief down. Sent it to join the mass already congealing in her belly. She could deal with it later. After it accrued to the point she could no longer stand upright.

"What…do you want, Sir?"

"Don't turn around."

"I wasn't planning on it."

"Good. I don't want to frighten your intended target. Prime gent. Looks tasty, if a bit cholesterol ridden for my taste."

"Is that why you're here? A meal?"

"Why wouldn't I be here? I think everyone's starting to descend on the city. It's a very happening place. Dark. Sinister. Steamy."

"That's probably the fog."

"Fog. Smoke. Mist. Whatever. London can be a creepy place. During the last millennia it was the largest city in the western world…and only second to Beijing. Did you know that?"

"So?"

"There's a lot to interest a body in London lately. Every amateur sleuth is booking a flight. And bringing the family. It's hard to find decent accommodations."

"So?" she said again.

"That sort of spotlight could be rather dangerous to a certain member of my organization. One…who just might have a death wish. So. I decided to do a quick check-up, among other things."

"You're here for me?"

"Smile at your meal, Cassandra. He's starting to wonder at your continuing interest in him."

She complied.

"They're here for Jack. You know that, don't you? Of course you do. It's all over the news. They all want to be here. It's like the Ripper has come back to life. Almost. It's a copycat. A very good one. With a few changes. The victims are all dead first. There's very little blood at the site. And this time around, the victims are male. They're found with the same wounds, however. Sliced. Dissected. Disemboweled. Certain portions removed. And oddly - of the three men - they've all been convicted felons. From all over the world. Here in London. Hmm. Murderers. Rapists. Set loose through some legal loophole or other contemporary issue. How…odd."

"So?" It was getting to be her instant answer. Easy. One word. Said without inflection.

"You know, the authorities claim to be stymied. They're doubling the force and considering outside help. I don't think they're entirely focused on the objective. They might not want to catch the killer just yet. Vigilantes are helpful at curbing crime. At first. And just look at the tourism it's generating."

"I hadn't noticed."

"Poor chaps. If they're stymied, it's not their fault. They haven't any promising leads. No prints. The DNA is inconclusive. Hmm. I rather wonder what a sample of our blood looks like under a microscope, don't you?"

"Not especially."

"I'm certain it's giving the forensics department over at Scotland Yard fits. What an amusing thought. I may have to check on it later."

"Sounds like I may have to help them. Send a message to the newspapers. Maybe, write on a wall," she answered.

"I'm worried about you, Cassandra. Suicide by cop is never acceptable, but you forgot to factor in the careers of the bobbies involved. That would be a shame, don't you think?"

"Who?"

"Imagine for a moment the scenario: London's finest officers have actually arrested the perpetrator of the Ripper copycat killings. They'll call in. They'll transport her to the 'Yard'. They could try and photographer her. They'll fail. Everything about this alleged murderess baffles them. And sooner or later, the sun will come up. She's not been turned long old enough for any UV immunity. She'll turn to dust in the handcuffs, her cell…why, she might even be heading to trial when it happens. And poof! There goes the copycat - escaping into Ripper lore. How is anyone going to explain that? And still keep their careers?"

"So?"

"You were never cruel, Cassandra. And I didn't save you from that randy peer and his friends just to watch you perish from a broken heart. Not if I can do anything about it."

Her eyes burned. She forced the emotion down. Concentrated. Stared. She didn't blink. She didn't move. Anything. Anywhere.

"Can I ask you something?"

She shrugged in reply. The satin rustled slightly.

"Does any of this help calm the rage?"

"Rage? Is that what you think?"

"I don't know what to think. That's one of the reasons I'm here. So tell me. If it's not rage…what?"

"Why do you want to know?"

"I've never met my mate, Cassandra. Despite the time involved. Do you realize how very lucky you are?"

"Lucky?"

Tears. Again. Damn him. She blinked helplessly and had to swipe at her cheeks when it didn't work. Damn him. Damn this. Damn everything. Vampires didn't cry. They didn't have emotions. They were cold. Dead. Why weren't any of her blocking techniques working?

"What would you call it?"

She sniffed. "You really want to know? All right, I'll tell you. It's complete and total blackness. I'm a hollow shell. A big, empty cavern that continually fills up with pain. And that's when I can control it. You got that? It's worse than any death. It has to be. And I have an entire eternity of it to face. Is that what you want to hear? Well?"

There was a scuffle sound coming from Akron's shadowed spot. Cassandra blocked it as she was everything else. It took a few moments before he spoke again. She used the time for composure. Strength.

"Oh. Darn. Look there. You took too long. Your target appears to have wearied of appealing to you. He's turned to another woman."

"There'll be another," she replied.

"Yes, there will. And another. And another. And is any of that going to help?"

She tossed her head. Adjusted her veil. Shifted the cell phone just slightly against the little signet ring, stifled the instant reaction. Wrapped it tightly to her.

"He phoned me, Cassie. That's really why I'm here."

"Who?"

"Jacob Walsh. Your mate."

She didn't answer. Something deep within her reacted. Pained. Burned.

"I'm embarrassed to admit it. He actually found us. Him, and that wizard crew of his. They got access around our security, using some embedded signal that's in our online site. And then he called me. Me. On my rotating private line that nobody knows. Shocked the hell out of just about everyone, myself included."

"Oh?"

She kept her tone even, her inflection noncommittal. Giving nothing away. She should've known it was wasted.

"He was in worse shape than you are, Cassandra. Much worse. Couldn't eat. Sleep. Wore the finish off his tile from pacing it. And he blamed me. Figures. He talks a lot, that mate of yours. Fast. Says I didn't give him enough time. I altered every perception of physics and didn't give him enough time to absorb the shock, gather data, and then make an informed decision. And back then he didn't know the real truth in the universe – love is all that matters."

She couldn't answer. Her voice choked off. Hearing about Jacob was bringing his image so close, she could almost feel him! And that made the mass in her belly swell somehow, and that put the grief too close to the surface. She should have bolted the moment Akron spoke up.

"You didn't tell...him where to f-f-find me, did you?" Oh no. She'd stuttered. That wasn't possible to hide.

"Of course not. I could barely get a word in edgewise, even if I'd wanted to. Doesn't take a fool to see why you didn't tell him about us. Not only is he very persuasive, but he believes continual speech is a great negotiation tactic to get a yes answer. I suppose if you're as smart as he is, it probably is."

She smiled slightly. The view blurred worse. She didn't have much time. Any longer and she was going to be prostrate with emotion that only her coffin witnessed.

"That fellow appears to have an inside track on world domination, and he doesn't care about any of it. Not anymore. He only cares about one thing. One. Hmm. I wonder what that could possibly be?"

She didn't answer. Her entire form was stiff. Still. Rapt.

"Oh, very well. I'll just tell you. I did what he asked. No. I shouldn't alter the facts so injudiciously. I did what that man begged, beseeched, and even offered his entire portfolio to pay me for."

"What?" The word was croaked. Unintelligible.

"I changed him. You should probably turn around now. I don't think I can keep him back much longer. Jake! Go gently. She's more fragile than even she knows. Small. Incredibly precious."

Cassandra spun, locked eyes with the most amazing sight in the world as Jake sped toward her, and a moment later she was in his arms. Up against his chest. Hugged. Enwrapped. Her legs encircled his hips. Perfectly fitted. At one with him again. If she really did have a heart, it was singing. Flying. Soaring.

"Oh Baby! Oh, Love. Forgive me. Oh, Cassie. I love you, Babe. I'm here. I'll always be here. Forever. You and me."

"Jacob?"

"In the flesh. Or…whatever."

There was a sinfully sexy vibe coming off him now. Altering the elements and enervating the air. Cassandra didn't know how she'd missed sensing it earlier. He was thinner, but it actually added rather than subtracted - sculpting the muscles she could feel. It also narrowed his face, but all she really saw were his olive green eyes glowing. And then his fangs as he grinned.

"When are you going to call me Jake?" he asked.

His face blurred with tears.

"Oh no. No tears, Babe. I'm here. We're together. Yes? Nothing's coming between us again. You hear? Nothing. I mean, if I can get over this undead thing, I'm pretty sure anything else is a given. Yes?"

"Oh…Jake." The name was sniffed, sobbed, and laughed.

He gave a whoop and spun with her. "You said it! You called me Jake. I heard you. Loud and—"

He would've said more. She didn't let him. She stopped him with a kiss. The moan that surged through them came from both throats. And then Akron's deep voice drifted across the alley to her.

"Ah. Love. And mating. Must be nice. Well…hello beautiful. May I join you? Buy you a drink? Escort you somewhere? You from here? Great city. What's your name, gorgeous? Mine's Akron. Akron Profit. No. No drink for me. I just stopped in for a quick bite…"

-o0o-

About the Author

Jackie is an Alaskan author who crafts full-length Scot Historical novels for Kensington, while moonlighting with her paranormal series: Vampire Assassin league, available in ebook and 2-pack paperbacks. She loves hearing from fans, who can contact her at www.jackieivie.com

www.ingramcontent.com/pod-product-compliance
Lightning Source LLC
Chambersburg PA
CBHW070818120626
46556CB00002B/564